HOPE Leaves

Jamaica

To my people and the land

KATE ELIZABETH ERNEST

Hope Leaves Jamaica

MAMMOTH

Acknowledgements

Day Oh! and *Sammy Dead Oh* from *Mango Spice* –
chosen by Yvonne Conolly,
Gloria Cameron and Sonia Singham
(A & C Black Publishers Ltd 1981),
reprinted by permission of A & C Black Publishers Ltd.

First published in Great Britain 1993
by Methuen Children's Books Ltd
Published 1994 by Mammoth
an imprint of Reed International Books Limited
Michelin House, 81 Fulham Road, London SW3 6RB
and Auckland and Melbourne

Reprinted 1995, 1996 (twice), 1997

Copyright © 1993 Kate Elizabeth Ernest

The right of Kate Elizabeth Ernest to be identified as author
of this work has been asserted by her in accordance with
the Copyright, Designs and Patents Act 1988

ISBN 0 7497 1693 2

A CIP catalogue record for this title
is available from the British Library

Printed and bound in Great Britain
by Cox & Wyman Ltd, Reading, Berkshire

Contents

1. The White Handkerchiefs 11
2. They Haven't Forgotten Us 18
3. First Day at School 26
4. Land We Love 34
5. The Legacy 41
6. Sweetie Man 50
7. Worshipping Two Masters 58
8. The Journey 64
9. Christmas Time Is Coming Soon 72
10. Waiting for the Harvest 78
11. Festival Time 86
12. The Storm 94
13. Treasures under the Tomb 101
14. Dominic 110
15. Hope Leaves Jamaica 118

Preface

In a move from town to country with a different voice, different clothes and a confusion about her situation, Hope finds she is more bewildered coming into attack. At school with their malice and 'blue-black skin glistening in the sun', skinny country girls turn on their bullying, trap-setting and persecution. It is a time of movement and change. It is a child's world at the mercy of adults. Daunted by a move to face a new school, new adults, new children, a popular boy dreads going to join his parents in England while his friends parch with envy. Hope would face this move too.

In a regular flow of proverbial sayings, in blended sounds of Africa and Britain, language adds its particular colour to the rural life. And, touchingly honest, with its emotions like thinking aloud, recollections record strong memories of a time and place. A warm landscape is peopled in a vibrant community spirit. While an emotional contribution for child or parent, *Hope Leaves Jamaica* is an autobiographical telling that offers entertaining information about a connection not yet familiar.

James Berry, November 1992

Foreword

I must say, when I first wrote *Hope Leaves Jamaica* I had taken it for granted that I was writing a story about a child growing up in rural Jamaica, detaching Hope from myself. This has since proved difficult! Also, at first I thought Great-Aunt Minnie was just another character, but now I know better. I feel a sense of pride, because it is as if these wonderful people are with me when I am writing.

I was the only one of four children who was born in the parish of St Ann, Jamaica, known as The Garden Parish because of the abundance of flowers. The other children were born in Kingston. We went to live in the country with our grandparents when our parents came to England. I was three years old at the time. I have no recollection of my mother, but I vaguely recall my father smiling constantly and he drove a huge car.

I was an introverted, perceptive child whom elderly people took to instantly. I adored my grandparents, especially my grandmother who was a higgler, market trader, in the Sixties. Often I accompanied her around the village as she sold her wares, women's underwear, and bought eggs, which she sold at the market in the capital of our parish, St Ann's Bay, which is about fifteen minutes drive from the famous Dunn's River Falls, situated in Ocho Rios, a tourist attraction on the north coast of the island.

I adored my grandmother's brother, my Great-Uncle Arthur, who rode past our house at sun-up, on his way to his field which was miles away from the village: you passed the ruin of old plantations, ancient cotton trees, stone walls, tall trees, wild animals, beautiful birds, especially hummingbirds, lazy-looking cattle drinking water from ponds and men planting yams and corn, singing folk songs as they worked, before you reached Uncle Arthur's field, hence I created Uncle Isaiah in the chapters Land We Love and Waiting For The Harvest as a tribute to him.

I was in awe of my Great-Grandmother Kate and my Great-Aunt Elizabeth, who were both housebound. They were very perceptive and fiercely proud of their people and the land, and they commanded a great deal of respect. I wrote The Legacy in memory of my Great-Grandmother Kate. Also, my Great-Aunt Elizabeth left me a silver spoon in her will. I still feel honoured because I was such a nervous, quiet child, I felt insignificant compared with all the other great-grand-nieces and nephews.

Sadly, I brought the spoon over from Jamaica, but it was mislaid when I was in my late teens. I wrote Treasures under the Tomb in memory of my Great-Aunt Elizabeth.

The village seemed cut off from civilization, but most people had radios, especially the young men who had been to America as casual labourers, and everyone listened to the BBC World News, knew all the popular songs, and loved dancing on the village green. It was a tight-knit community.

Most of the villagers were regular church-goers and they knew all the sacred songs and the elders quoted freely from the Bible. The pastor was a revered figure in the community and he loved thumping the pulpit whilst preaching. I can still recall some amusing incidents as we sat listening to the pastor, such as a horse neighing, a donkey braying in the churchyard, a parishioner tripping on the polished floor as he entered the church, causing others to giggle, and the elderly parishioners were always dozing off and snoring. I have tried to recapture those moments in my stories.

I was five years old when Jamaica gained her independence. There was a show of nationalism all over the country, and our village was no exception. However, not everyone believed in singing their hearts out or pledging their loyalty to Jamaica; many people felt that it would take a miracle to improve Jamaica overnight, and so

I wrote Festival Time.

The 1950s and the early 1960s were a time of upheaval for families in the West Indies. Lack of work and limited opportunity forced many people to leave the islands to seek a better break in England or America. As a result, many families were split up indefinitely. I hope that Hope's memories of a Jamaican country childhood with grandparents would be shared by many other children.

1

The White Handkerchiefs

'Where is Mother?' I asked.

We were standing by the Chevrolet outside our house, which was all boarded up.

Father settled us into the car and said, 'Your mother is in the country.'

I had not questioned Mother's disappearance before because she was always going to the country for a rest. One time she had returned home with a yelling baby boy, Joshua. Now we were excited because we thought we were going to see Mother, who was staying with Father's parents in the country. We waved goodbye to the neighbours and Peaches, who had been looking after us but had now found another job.

The car sped off. We left Kingston and travelled up winding mountain roads, looking down at ferns, frothing rivers and huge boulders of rocks in the many ravines along the way. Occasionally, on either side of the dusty roads, ancient trees spread their branches like canopies, blotting out the sunlight.

We came to a sharp bend and a bus blared its horn. Father pulled over and we held our breath. We were on the edge of a precipice where burnt-out vehicles lay on their sides below us. We thought the car would roll into the ravine. The bus driver continued honking the horn until the bus, which was full of noisy market women, was out of sight. We were safe.

Ruth and Joshua fell asleep. Father slowed down and wiped his face with a white handkerchief. Then he silently stared ahead as the cool breeze wafted into the car. I sensed he did not want to talk. The road led downward and we passed a small village where people stared at us as if we were tourists. Finally, we entered the countryside where stone walls stretched for miles, twisting with the narrow lanes, and cattle grazed in green pastures.

We approached a crossroads and Father turned into a narrow lane. Coffee and citrus trees were in bloom; the scent lingered in the air. We stopped outside a small cottage with a verandah to the front. Gideon, the horse, was drinking water from a trough near by. This was where our grandparents lived.

Grandma Rhoda was of medium height. She had tiny warts at the corner of her eyes and her hair was hidden under a red headscarf. She enjoyed singing Gospel songs, and would break into a singsong at odd times, turning each song into a medley. Then she encouraged us all to join in.

Grandpa Noah had broad shoulders and hands that were roughened with hard work. He was kind and gentle and he had a gold tooth which glistened whenever he smiled. He was also fond of dancing and often did a jig, which made us giggle. He enjoyed woodwork and he had carved several boats for the pastor, who had named them the *Nina*, the *Pinta* and the *Santa Maria*, after Christopher Columbus's ships.

The cottage was painted cream. It sat on its white-washed foundation where a cellar door was exposed to one side. It had jalousie windows and steps leading up to the verandah where red speckled tiles were always cool to the touch. Two rocking-chairs lived there. Grandma and Grandpa spent most evenings relaxing in their chairs and watched the passers-by.

'Children,' Father said, 'it seems you've all been struck dumb. Mind your manners. Go and greet your grandparents.'

Ruth and Joshua had been staring at a small black lizard, a Polly lizard, sunning itself on the side of the verandah. We snapped from our trance and climbed the steps of the verandah to greet our grandparents. We were so pleased to see them that we did not realise that Mother was not sitting with them.

'Children,' our grandparents said, 'you've arrived just in time for lunch. You must be hot and thirsty.'

After lunch, Father talked about the presents

he was going to buy us for Christmas: a harmonica for Joshua, a mirror for Ruth and a big doll for me. He passed three handkerchiefs to Ruth, who loved pleating them. After she had finished pleating them, she always placed two in his shirt pockets and the other in the back pocket of his trousers.

'Children,' Father said, 'be good for your grandparents.' He kissed Grandma. She squeezed his hand. Then he shook hands with Grandpa, who patted him on the back. Father had eaten a big meal, which seemed strange because he had been picking at his food for days. He said he was off to buy candy, which made me think he was definitely acting strange. He never allowed us to eat sweets, not even on special days and there was nothing special about today. He kissed us and hugged us, rocking us from side to side. Then he drove off, tooting the horn along the lane.

I was worried because I suddenly realised that Father was dressed as if he was going to church, though it was a Wednesday afternoon. He never wore a dark suit and a felt hat on Wednesdays. There was something about Father's behaviour that troubled me deeply. Nevertheless, I brushed aside my fears and joined the others, chasing after the car.

'Father, Father, are you going to collect Mother?' we shouted. We thought Mother had gone to see her old friend, the postmistress. She always visited the post office whenever she was in the country. Mother was an orphan and an outsider. She had come to the village to work at the post office. She had sold Father some stamps, and they were married a year later.

''Kerchief . . .' Joshua pointed at Ruth's right hand.

'He's gone off without them,' Ruth said in disbelief. 'Father, Father,' she shouted, waving the white handkerchiefs frantically. But Father had picked up speed and our voices were inaudible as the car tyres crunched on gravel, leaving a cloud of dust behind.

We came to a halt, panting. The dust blinded us and the car disappeared. We felt cheated because we had always chased after the car whenever Father left us in the country. He would stop and lean out of the car window and say, 'Children, I shan't be long. Be good for your grandparents.'

Ruth sniffed the crisp handkerchiefs. The pleats were undone. She burst into tears. 'Why didn't Father stop? He knows we always chase after him.'

Joshua began to cough because of the dust. He held out his little hand to me. Ruth walked alongside. Something was wrong, but we still did not know what it was. I took Joshua's hand and tried to comfort him and Ruth. 'Oh well, we'll give them to Father later.'

'Perhaps Mother will tell us the story of

Hansel and Gretel tonight,' Ruth said. 'We haven't heard it for ages.'

'Where's Mother?' Joshua wailed. 'I'm tired and I want her to tuck me up in bed right now.'

I held his hand really tightly as we turned and slowly headed towards the cottage. I couldn't tell him what I now suspected: that Mother wouldn't be there when we got back. I was right. But Grandma and Grandpa were waiting with open arms to hug us, saying, 'Never mind, children. It won't be long before you see your parents again.'

The warmth of our grandparents' bodies enveloped us, but deep down we were doubtful, because the statement 'It won't be long . . .' seemed like an eternity to us: I was seven, Ruth was five and Joshua was only four.

That night, we observed the cottage as if for the first time. The sitting-room also doubled as the dining-room. There was a small mahogany writing-desk, a display cabinet, full of delicate china, and a dining-table and four chairs. There was also a large cabinet where Grandma stored her groceries.

We sat round the dining-table listening to duppy-stories until Joshua began to yawn. He was sitting on Grandpa's lap. Grandpa carried him into a tiny room and tucked him into bed.

'Don't leave me, Grandpa,' Joshua said. 'I'm scared of the dark. I want to sleep with Ruth and Hope!'

'Noah,' Grandma called after Grandpa, 'you've frightened the child with your duppy-stories.' She added, 'All right, Joshua. You can sleep with the girls until you feel confident enough to sleep on your own.'

We children finally settled down in a large, creaking bed where we huddled together under a patchwork quilt.

'Grandma,' Joshua said, 'can you tell us a fairy-story?'

'When I was a boy,' Grandpa said, 'I used to love sitting under a big tamarind tree at dusk, listening to folk tales.'

Grandpa held the gas lamp while Grandma said, 'You children know far too many fairy-stories. Tonight I'm going to tell you an Anancy-story.'

2

They Haven't Forgotten Us

We had been in the country for a whole week and had cried ourselves to sleep every night. We still thought Father had collected Mother in the village and had returned to Kingston without us. We wondered what was taking them so long to come and fetch us, and voiced our thoughts. But our grandparents always said, 'Settle down, children. You'll be with your parents soon.'

'When will that be?' I asked one day, as I watched Grandma embroidering a white sheet. She sat in her rocking-chair, rocking as she worked. She was wearing glasses. They kept slipping, so she wrinkled her nose in order to push them up.

'When the time is right,' she said firmly, and I could hear her breathing heavily as she looked away.

I thought my parents had abandoned me and I felt sorry for myself. But I also felt sorry for Grandma because I sensed that something bad had happened and she had been sworn to secrecy. She turned to me and smiled. 'Be a good girl, Hope. Fetch me a handkerchief. My glasses are dirty.'

Grandpa had promised to take us on a picnic down in the pasture where he kept the horses. But right now he was feeding his horse, Gideon, who was dark brown with big, rolling eyes. Grandma could not accompany us because she was busy baking cakes for the ladies in the church choir in which she sang. She looked so sad as she got up and hunched her shoulders, that I did not dare ask her any more questions. I went to fetch the handkerchief. Afterwards I joined the others in the yard.

Grandpa helped Ruth and Joshua on to Gideon's back. Then he did a jig, saying, 'Hold on tight, you two.' He whispered in Gideon's ear. The horse showed its teeth, then reared up, neighing, while Ruth and Joshua screamed with fright.

'Noah.' Grandma smiled at last. 'Sometimes you behave worse than a child.' She sighed. 'That's a dangerous thing to do. The children could fall off and hurt themselves.'

We waved goodbye to Grandma. Grandpa led Gideon down the lane while I walked alongside. We children wore straw hats and jeans tucked into wellingtons. Grandpa carried a lasso and a food container, consisting of four aluminium bowls which were stacked on top of each other. The lasso hung from Grandpa's left shoulder. He looked big and upright as he walked briskly, wearing jeans tucked into gum boots.

'Grandpa,' Ruth said, looking all around, 'this place is very lonely. It reminds me of the story of Hansel and Gretel.'

'You are not going to leave us in the forest, are you, Grandpa?' Joshua stared at ancient cotton trees.

'Whatever gave you that idea?' Grandpa chuckled. His voice was carried on the wind. 'Hansel and Gretel, eh!' He laughed louder. 'That's just a fairy-story, children.'

Ruth decided to walk the rest of the way. She kept stopping. First she wanted to look at a bird's nest. Then she picked wild berries and threw them to the birds. Later she stopped under a guava tree and ate guavas. Her soft jet-black hair was caught up in a ponytail which could swing to and fro like Gideon's tail.

When we reached the corral, Grandpa showed us the horses. There were Shiloh, the stallion, Windsome, Star and Eartha, the mares, and the two colts, Samson and Jubal. The mares stood in one corner, neighing, while Shiloh galloped round and round. Samson, Jubal and Shiloh were jet-black and fierce. They reared up and stamped their front hooves, whinnying, trying to attract Gideon's attention.

Two hired hands tended the horses. Man-Man and Big-Man were twins. They had been to America, where they had worked as casual labourers. Man-Man was big with wide shoulders. He wore a blue bandanna round his neck and also wore crinkly leather boots, in which he had tucked his torn denims. Big-Man wore a khaki boiler suit, tucked into leather boots. He perspired openly and used a yellow bandanna to wipe his face.

'Howdy, folks.' Man-Man took off his bandanna, which he used to wipe his perspiring face. 'The mares are with foal again,' he addressed Grandpa. Then he winked at us.

Grandpa helped Joshua down from Gideon's back. Joshua's big dark eyes took up so much of his little face. We walked over to the corral and the horses galloped towards the fence. They neighed excitedly and Grandpa said: 'Samson, Jubal, Shiloh, stop fussing and come and meet my grandchildren.'

'The mares haven't been exercised today,' Big-Man said. 'Perhaps the children would like to lead them around.'

'Can we, Grandpa?' Joshua asked. Even his ears showed his excitement. His ears stuck out and Father had said they reminded him of a cast-iron cooking pot with two arms akimbo.

'Please say yes, Grandpa.' Ruth tugged at Grandpa's arm.

'Only for a short while,' Grandpa said. 'The mares are with foal and I don't want them getting excited.'

'Do you mean they are allowed to play with fowls?' Ruth asked, looking rather confused.

'The mares are expecting,' Grandpa chuckled.

'Gideon has earned his keep; he's mated successfully with the mares.'

Gideon grazed alongside Jubal, Samson and Shiloh. He shook his mane, whinnied and nuzzled the horses – he was their father. Then they all cantered off.

Grandpa allowed Ruth to lead Windsome round the corral. Big-Man stayed with Joshua, leading Eartha round and round while I gingerly held Star's lead and trotted alongside. The mares were all brown, though Star had a white patch between her eyes. She nuzzled me and I cringed. But Man-Man said: 'Horses are very gentle, providing you treat them right. Go on, pat her. She won't bite you.'

Grandpa decided that the horses were in a good mood, so we were allowed to ride them for a short while. We cantered out into the pasture and the men walked alongside, discussing the expected foals.

'Grandpa,' Joshua said, 'please let me have my own horse.'

'Me too, Grandpa,' Ruth said. 'I don't want the mirror that Father promised me for Christmas.'

I was really surprised. This was amazing for Ruth. Father used to say when Ruth stared at her reflection in Mother's mirror that the mirror would crack one day, and there would be seven years' bad luck. But she was too vain to mind!

'You children can ride the horses whenever

you like,' Grandpa said, 'but you can't have the foals. I breed them to sell. That is how I make my living, along with the farm produce and the livestock on the farm.'

We had never thought about how our grandparents made their living before. Now we understood.

The sun was high above. Wild flowers danced in the breeze, farmers waved at us as they made their way to their fields, cows mooed far off and our bodies jerked in unison with the cantering horses.

We stopped under a lime tree with the distinctive scent of lime around us. Grandpa said it was time for our picnic. We thought we would be eating from the aluminium containers, but Grandpa had fooled us; they were empty.

Man-Man and Big-Man went to see to the horses. Meantime, we sat back wondering what had happened to the food. We got a big surprise when Grandma joined us. She had misled us into thinking that she was baking cakes for the ladies in the church choir. She carried a basket full of fried chicken, sandwiches, fruit, biscuits shaped like animals, and a variety of small cakes made of ginger or coconut.

Grandpa spread out the white sheet that Grandma had been embroidering with flowers. We said our grace. Then we ate. Afterwards we stretched out on the sheet on the grass and put our worries behind us. We so loved our grandparents.

'Grandma,' Joshua announced, 'you are the best person in the whole world. You too, Grandpa.' He hugged them, adding, 'But can I please have one of the foals? I really want a pet.'

'We'll get you something that you really want,' Grandpa said. He went off swinging the handle of the creaking aluminium container; he had filled it with food for the men.

Grandma cleared up while we watched her. 'I found these on the way here,' she said, holding three white handkerchiefs.

Ruth said very solemnly: 'I thought Grandpa was going to leave us in the forest, so I used them to mark the way, just like in Hansel and Gretel when the children marked their way home after their father took them into the forest.'

'Children,' Grandma reassured us, 'your grandpa and I love you. We would never let anything bad happen to you.'

Grandpa was smiling when he returned. He handed us each a small parcel, wrapped in shiny silver paper, the kind Mother always used. 'These are from your parents. Your father left them with us.'

'But it's not Christmas.' I stared at a white doll with brown hair. It blinked and was able to stand up by itself.

'So they haven't forgotten us,' Ruth said, admiring her face in an oval mirror which had a tortoiseshell handle.

'A mouth organ!' Joshua began to blow the red harmonica.

'Children,' Grandma said, 'we know Christmas is a long way off, but we wanted to put the smile back on your faces.'

'This is from your grandma and me.' Grandpa gave us each a wooden horse. He had carved and varnished Shiloh, Samson and Jubal, especially for us, before we arrived in the country.

We proudly examined our gifts until a flock of small white-bellied birds surrounded us. They sang tirelessly as they searched for food.

'Shoo!' Grandma exclaimed. 'Noisy little things.'

Grandpa smiled and said, 'Children, listen carefully. These birds are called Johnchewits because of the sound they make.' He sang huskily: 'Johnchewit, Johnchewit . . .'

Grandma gathered up the remains of our lunch and folded up the sheet. Then we all fed the birds and sang: 'Johnchewit, Johnchewit . . .' At last we were beginning to enjoy the freedom of the countryside.

3

First Day at School

Soon we received another parcel and a letter, this time from England. Ruth and I now knew that our parents were no longer in Jamaica, though Joshua was unaware of this new discovery. Our grandparents felt that for the time being it was best for him to think Mother and Father would be back shortly. Even though England was mentioned often, he thought it was a place in Kingston.

The school term was about to begin. Ruth and I were to attend the local primary school, while Joshua stayed at home with Grandma. Ruth was looking forward to going to school. She had made friends at Sunday school, and they would all be starting school together. But I was not looking forward to going, not one little bit, because many of the children at Sunday school had taken a dislike to me. The parcel we had received contained English clothes and most of the girls of my age were already dead jealous of me. The clothes would make it worse.

It was raining the day school started. We stood on the verandah, watching the drizzle. I prayed that the rain would fall so hard all day that we could stay at home. Grandma had dressed us in pale-blue checked dresses, new T-bar shoes and white ankle socks. There were crisp ribbons in our hair.

'I'm glad your mother sent these raincoats and umbrellas, girls,' Grandma said. 'Now there's no chance of your uniforms getting wet.'

Grandpa smiled as Grandma helped us into our raincoats. 'You girls will be the envy of the whole school.' He held out our leather satchels. 'My, my, you two sure look smart. You remind me of real English schoolchildren.'

'Can I go with them?' Joshua asked, turning up his little face to Grandpa. 'I don't want to be left alone.'

'But you'll have me for company,' Grandma said. 'We'll go and see if there are any letters at the post office later on.'

The rain eased up and Grandma breathed a sigh of relief, saying, 'Come along, girls. Let's get going.'

We walked along the main road. The water had soaked away, though there were puddles in craters. The culverts were full of leaves and raindrops glistened on the tiny green leaves of vines that grew on the stone walls. There was the sound of a motor vehicle. Grandma looked behind and said, 'Thank you, Lord. You've answered my prayers. Here comes Mr Brown.'

A van pulled up, bearing the words United Bakeries. The driver, a balding man with a gold tooth, got out and opened a sliding door. Grandma sat up front. Ruth and I sat in the back. Our stomachs rumbled and the van jolted on the bumpy road as the scent of freshly baked bread, Bulla cakes and buns filled our nostrils.

When we arrived at the school gates, Mr Brown tooted the horn. He waved us off, saying he would give us a lift in the mornings. Some of the schoolchildren hungrily licked their lips while others glared at us enviously, for Mr Baker never carried schoolchildren in his van. It was as if we were important visitors. We realized we were exceptional. It must have been because our grandparents were highly thought of, our grandpa was such a big man.

The playground was slightly raised with the school in the background. The grass was worn away in places. There was a huge rainwater tank and a plot at the far corner, where the boys cultivated all types of vegetables. There were plum and apple trees scattered around. One area was reserved for playing cricket and another for volley ball.

'The headmaster is expecting us.' Grandma took hold of our hands. 'There he is,' she added, leading us up a flight of concrete steps which seemed to go on for ever.

'Please don't leave us, Grandma!' I wailed, while Ruth walked confidently at Grandma's side.

Mr Trelawny, the headmaster, was a stout

28

man with greying hair and whiskers. His opening words were, 'Children, welcome to our school. I'm a strict disciplinarian, but I'm also very fair.' He exchanged words with Grandma, and then she left us.

Ruth eagerly went off to her class. I entered mine. All the other children sat and stared at me.

After morning assembly and roll call, the teacher greeted us with, 'Good morning, children.'

'Good morning, Miss Clover,' the children chanted.

Miss Clover, like all the other teachers, wore a hobble skirt, a crisp white blouse and a shiny belt round her tiny waist. Her long neck reminded me of a bottle. Her hair was combed back and put up with hair grips. Several bangles jangled on her wrists. She looked up, saying, 'I would like someone to stand up and read aloud.'

There was no volunteer, so Miss Clover chose me. Anyway, she said she had taught the same class the previous year so she had heard them all read aloud before. I got up and turned the pages of a brand-new poetry book belonging to Miss Clover. I recited in a trembling voice: 'The Sands of Dee, by Charles Kingsley. Oh Mary, go and call the cattle home, and call the cattle home, across the sands of Dee . . .'

'Well done,' Miss Clover said. 'Now pass the

book to Precious. Let's see who's the best reader in my class.'

A skinny girl arose, glaring at me. Her hair was plaited, like rows of corn. She lowered her eyes and recited: 'The rolling tide came in and hit the land, and never home came she. Oh, is it reed, or floating hair? A tress of golden hair, a drown-ed maiden's hair . . .'

'Enough.' Miss Clover held up a hand, adding: 'Not bad, Precious, but you should have continued where Hope left off.'

Precious glared at me again as the children took turns to read aloud. She leaned and whispered to her friends until Miss Clover looked up. Then the bell sounded throughout the school.

At break, I stood alone in the playground because I couldn't find Ruth. I watched a group of girls skipping and I longed to join in. They sang, 'London Bridge is falling . . .' as they skipped. I noticed that Precious was the ring leader. She encouraged her friends to make faces and to poke out their tongues at me.

'We don't like outsiders,' Precious shouted. She stopped skipping and approached me. She poked my shoulder, saying: 'My mama says you are a waif and we don't want you here.' She pushed me and I fell backwards in the dirt.

'Ah, ah, ah,' the voices crowed at me. 'Your pretty uniform is soiled now. Look at all that mud!'

I got up, sniffing. Precious tugged at my hair, throwing my ribbon into the dirt, laughing: 'Ah, ah, ah.'

'Cry baby, cry baby . . .' the voices shrieked. 'We don't want you here. You're a show-off and a Kingstonian!' They poked my shoulders really hard and I fled towards the classroom.

Miss Clover said: 'I'm afraid country children don't take kindly to city children, especially when they are dressed like an English schoolgirl. Your grandma should get you a proper school uniform: navy pleated skirt, short-sleeved white blouse and black plimsolls.' Then she added, 'From tomorrow I want you to stay in the schoolyard at recess-time.'

'Yes, Miss Clover,' I said, just as the bell went. Then the classroom filled with noisy children. I went back to my seat feeling unwelcome. Somehow I got through that first day.

That night, after we had had supper, Grandma and Grandpa asked what had happened to my uniform and my ribbon? So I told them about the bullies.

'Children,' Grandpa said, 'your family has lived in this village since the days of slavery. You have every right to be here. You are descended from a tall African tribe who loved music and dancing. They were skilled in woodcraft. You should be proud of them. I've inherited the skill from my Great-Grandfather

Tembi. Don't let these silly girls upset you.'

'Grandpa,' Joshua said, 'I'm glad I'm not old enough to go to school. I want to stay home with you and Grandma for ever.'

Grandma refused to buy us new uniforms. 'Your checked dresses are much cooler than the pleated navy skirts and your T-bar shoes are hardwearing. I'm not going to spend money if I don't need to.'

'Please buy me a new uniform, Grandma,' Ruth pleaded. 'My friends won't like me if I look different from them.'

Grandpa rose from the table, picking up the gas lamp. He shone it in our faces. 'Children, if your friends can't accept you as you are, they are not worthy of being called friends.'

'That's right, children,' Grandma said. 'But I'll speak to the headmaster tomorrow. This bullying has to stop and it's time you children learned about your family history. We are firmly rooted in this village!'

'The pastor says I resemble one of my great-aunts,' Ruth declared. 'And everyone says Hope's going to be serene and studious like Grandpa's mama, Granny Keziah.'

'I'm not an outsider!' Joshua protested. 'Everyone says my ears stick out like Grandpa's papa's ears used to.'

Grandpa smiled: 'Joshua, boy, you've certainly inherited Papa 'Zekiel's ears, such a big man. Why, Papa was even taller than me.

Let's hope you don't grow to be as tall as he was. We don't want any more giants in this family.'

'Grandpa,' Joshua said, 'do giants really eat children?'

'Nah.' Grandpa licked his lips playfully. 'But this giant does.' He chased us round the room, roaring: 'Fee, fi, fo, fum, I smell the blood of three little children . . .'

We children fled into our bedroom giggling, followed by Grandma. We went off to bed happy and exhausted. We knew that we truly belonged in the village. I also hoped there would be no more bullying at school because the children were afraid of Mr Trelawny. I drifted off to sleep, thinking, I'm looking forward to my second day at school.

4

Land We Love

Our first few weeks in the country were made easier by Grandma's brother, Uncle Isaiah. There was not much for us to do on Saturdays so we often accompanied Uncle Isaiah to his field. He rode past our cottage on his huge black stallion, Cheyenne. He always wore a freshly ironed khaki boiler suit, and was a lanky man with a smile just like Grandma's.

'Children,' Uncle Isaiah said, one morning, 'see if your grandpa will let you borrow old Gideon for the day.'

Grandpa stood by Gideon's trough, drinking herbal tea from an enamel mug. 'Morning, Isaiah,' he said. 'Cheyenne reminds me of Jubal: fierce and fiery.' He looked down at us, saying: 'All right, but watch out for rat traps, they're all over the place, and mind Gideon's hooves; I've only just shoed him.'

Grandma handed us our straw hats and our water containers while Grandpa seated us on Gideon. Then we set off, saying: 'Giddy-up, Gideon, giddy-up . . .'

After a long journey through green pastures and fields, where we waved at men planting rows of yam hills and tobacco, Uncle Isaiah announced, 'Children, it's time old Gideon had a rest.'

We walked alongside Gideon. Vultures searched for carrion, woodpeckers pecked at tall cedar trees and rats the size of kittens, roamed in the bushes while fruits hung from thin branches, there were naseberries and sweetsops. There was a river near by and we watched the water rushing endlessly on.

We reached Uncle Isaiah's field. Wild rabbits and rats scurried into the bushes. Lizards crawled down tall cedar trees, darting in and out of holes which were made by woodpeckers. A mongoose sat staring at us. Uncle Isaiah stamped his feet. 'Off with you, sly mongoose! You're supposed to be catching rats. After all, that's why your ancestors were brought over from India in the first place.'

'You should have caught it.' Joshua frowned. 'I could have kept it as a pet.'

'Mongeese prefer to live in the wild and they eat hens if they get the chance,' Uncle Isaiah said. 'You should get a kitten instead.'

Later, Uncle Isaiah tended his vegetables: cassavas, tomatoes, Irish potatoes and sweet corn. We knelt on the earth, weeding cornflower and fussing over corn stalks, for some of the corn had been eaten by rats and parakeets.

Gideon and Cheyenne grazed side by side.

They swung their tails to and fro, getting rid of flies and birds as they wandered off. Harvest time was approaching and Uncle Isaiah had set traps for wild animals. He also made a scarecrow to fool the parakeets that continuously stole the corn, and the tame doves that cooed and ate from our hands.

At noon Uncle Isaiah stopped for lunch. 'Children,' he said, 'what would your parents say if they could see you now? You look like real country children.' He stared at an aeroplane, high above. 'My only son Samuel and the grandchildren are in America. I wish I could see them, but I'm too old to travel now.'

'What's taking Mother and Father so long to come and get us?' Joshua asked, sitting back and leaning on a tree trunk.

'Ah, Joshua, boy,' Uncle Isaiah said, sighing. 'One day you will understand.'

This answer seemed to be enough for Joshua.

'One day we'll be together,' Ruth said, confidently.

I was tired of the long wait and somehow I had lost faith in my parents, but I did not voice my thoughts.

Uncle Isaiah produced enamel plates and mugs from a hessian sack which he had tied to Cheyenne's saddle. He had cooked Irish potatoes and corn on the cob, as well as opening a tin of red herrings. He passed the plates around, saying, 'Eat up, children.' Then we sat and ate under a guinep tree. We also drank a refreshing cordial made from the limes that grew all around and water from our containers, adding molasses from Uncle Isaiah's saddle-bag.

'Uncle Isaiah,' Ruth asked, as the red ants marched like soldiers round our feet while we ate. 'Why has this family got so much land, yet others have none?'

'Manners,' he said. 'Don't talk with your mouth full, child.' He rose and put out the fire.

Joshua shelled a corn cob and fed the ground doves. Then he stood by the scarecrow with its outstretched arms, wearing Uncle Isaiah's hat, which had a tobacco smell to it, for Uncle Isaiah also planted tobacco. Uncle Isaiah bundled firewood, ready to place on Cheyenne's litter. Cheyenne and Gideon grazed side by side under a lime tree. They often flapped their ears and swung their tails to and fro to get rid of the flies.

Uncle Isaiah looked up and said, 'Children, hard work is the only way to succeed. That is why our family has land. Hard work.'

Gideon neighed and galloped towards us, stamping his hooves as he halted by the hot ashes of the dying fire. From afar, Cheyenne neighed and reared up. Uncle Isaiah ran and we followed. There was a terrible squeaking sound and we stared at a mouse in horror.

'I've caught one of the little devils,' Uncle Isaiah said.

There was more squeaking. We saw at least

six mice scurrying away. Their mother had been caught in a trap. We pleaded with Uncle Isaiah to let her go, but he refused.

'The babies will all die of starvation!' Ruth wailed.

'That's the object of it.' Uncle Isaiah clapped his hand. 'Then they'll stop eating the corn.'

Gideon and Cheyenne reared, with their manes standing. They seemed agitated. The mouse was caught by its tail. It dragged the trap along, twisting and struggling.

'Please, Uncle Isaiah,' Joshua wailed. 'Please spare its life, otherwise the babies will die.'

Uncle Isaiah had a gleeful look on his face. 'Children, survival is for the fittest. Rodents cause a lot of damage. If I let it live, it will breed again. Then we are the ones that will starve. No. It has to die.'

'Do it for us, Uncle Isaiah,' I cried, tugging at his arm. 'We are motherless and fatherless at the moment. We don't want the same thing to happen to the poor babies.' There was a note of desperation in my voice. I had surprised myself as I blurted out these words. Now I was ashamed of my behaviour.

Uncle Isaiah's face softened. 'All right. But you children must understand that all rodents are pests. They can and will destroy a whole crop of corn.' He walked over to the struggling mouse and reluctantly freed it.

The remainder of the time passed in silence.

Uncle Isaiah secured the firewood on Cheyenne's litter. The fire was doused. The hessian sack was placed on the saddle. Then we children mounted Gideon with relief. We were going home at last, distancing ourselves from this horrible scene.

When we were in sight of home, Uncle Isaiah said: 'Children, I'm sorry I upset you today, but if you are to settle in the country, you must accept that certain animals and insects are a danger to man's livelihood.'

Our grandparents were waiting at the gate to greet us. But this time they weren't smiling and their arms hung limply at their sides. 'Children, thank God you're home. We need cheering up. What a day we've had!'

Grandpa patted Gideon's side as we dismounted. 'Children, your grandma is heartbroken. Her favourite hen died today.' (Frizzle was a white hen with an abundance of feathers. She laid all the eggs that we ate.)

'A huge hawk picked her up and flew off,' Grandma said, sniffing. 'But she was too heavy, so it dropped her from a great height. She died instantly.'

'It took us ages to find her,' Grandpa said, 'and as we approached, we saw a mongoose dragging her into the bushes.'

'You should have killed the mongoose!' Joshua exclaimed.

Uncle Isaiah said, 'Children, now you

39

understand why I wanted to kill that mouse today. We can't have these animals stealing our livestock and damaging our crops now, can we?'

We were stunned. We could not believe that the white frizzly hen, Grandma's champion egg-layer, had gone for ever. We clung to our grandparents, comforting them.

'Children,' Grandma said, 'I'm afraid there'll be no more eggs for breakfast. It will be cornmeal porridge from now on.'

'Poor old Frizzle,' Ruth said. 'No more eggs for breakfast?' She frowned. 'I hate cornmeal porridge!'

Joshua separated from the group. He watched a hawk flying above. 'Grandpa,' he asked, 'can you show me how to set a calaban? We can't have all these pests taking away our food!'

5

The Legacy

Most Sundays we went walkabout in the village, passing higglers who sold household goods and novelties, until we reached Uncle Isaiah's house which was built on a hill.

'Hope,' Uncle Isaiah said, one peaceful Sunday afternoon, 'you resemble your Great-Grandmother Sadie, though she was fair skinned. She had the same big dark eyes.' He rose and spread his arms, saying, 'Children, all that you see belongs to this family. Your ancestors were pioneers.'

Ruth thought he meant buccaneers. She said, 'Do you mean they stole all this land?'

'No. Children, your ancestors worked their fingers to the bone, toiling come rain or shine, so that this land could be ours.' Uncle Isaiah cracked his knuckles.

There were tears in Joshua's eyes as he looked above the hillside, down into the valley and to where the Blue Mahoe trees seemed to be touching the sky. The rain was falling in the distance, yet there was no rainfall where we were.

'I can't bear to think of them working in the

rain,' Joshua wailed. 'To think they shed all that blood for us.'

'Joshua,' Uncle Isaiah said, 'you must not take everything you hear for gospel.'

'I'll never know what to believe!' Joshua declared.

'Isaiah,' Grandma said, 'you've really cherished this place. Children, I was born in this house.'

The large brick-fronted house, with its verandah, had withstood several hurricanes. Uncle Isaiah had looked after it well. It stood on a hill where a twisted path led from the blue and white house all the way down into the valley, joining the main road.

Uncle Isaiah's wife, Aunt Enid, was a tall slender woman, who always wore a blue dress and a gingham apron. She was an outsider and she had come to the village to marry Uncle Isaiah. Perhaps being an outsider was why she never spoke much. She joined us on the verandah. I stared at her fair skin, which looked red, as she handed us each a glass of soda pop. Her brown eyes followed us, but as usual she said nothing and quickly returned to the sitting-room.

Grandma looked at us and said: 'Children, sit still and don't touch anything. Your Aunt Enid is houseproud, so I want you to be as good as gold.'

'Does that mean we will be like Midas?' Ruth

asked. 'We have been sitting still for ages.'

'I hope not,' Grandma chuckled. 'I don't fancy you children turning to gold.'

'Then we'd have to scrub your skin to the bones.' Uncle Isaiah laughed. Then he sobered up and said: 'There's no doubt about it; our people were certainly pioneers.'

'But if they were slaves,' Joshua asked, 'how could they have been pioneers? Is a pioneer the same as a buccaneer?'

'Aaragh, Joshua, lad,' Uncle Isaiah said with humour. 'The life of a slave was not always one of toil. There was also merrymaking in the village square on Saturday nights.'

Grandma stared at an annatto tree near by with prickly pods hanging down. 'Children,' she said, pointing, 'that tree was planted when I was a child. It reminds me of my sisters; only Aunt Esmé is still alive.' (Aunt Esmé's grandson Robin was my only friend at school.) Grandma sighed. 'When Esmé and I were young we picked annatto to add colour to sauces.' Then she turned to her brother: 'Isaiah, this land of ours must never be sold. It must be handed down to your son Samuel.'

'Rhoda, I long to see that boy,' Uncle Isaiah said and stared hard at Cheyenne grazing in the yard.

Like most of the villagers, Grandma came from a large family. She had another brother, Uncle Lincoln, who lived in a distant village.

Her Aunt Minnie, our great-aunt, lived with Uncle Isaiah and Aunt Enid. She was taking a nap as we sat drinking soda pop and listening to Uncle Isaiah and Grandma remembering their youth. Suddenly, there was the sound of rustling inside the house. Then a stern voice called out: 'Isaiah, I'm hungry and I'm thirsty; do something about it.'

Great-Aunt Minnie was now awake. She was the oldest member of our family. She was tall and dark with broken stumps of teeth. She suffered from toothache and earache and smelled of cloves and camphorated oil. We filed into the sitting-room where she was brought out by Uncle Isaiah and Aunt Enid. Uncle Isaiah patiently fed her with mashed cho-chos and steamed fish. Then Aunt Enid held a glass of carrot juice to her mouth.

'Rhoda,' Great-Aunt Minnie said, 'my eyesight is fading; bring the children closer. I want to smell their skin and touch their faces.' When she was satisfied that she recognized each of us, she spoke. 'Ruth, you are the prettiest. You take after Great-Aunt Lilian who was a mulatto.'

She poked Ruth's eyes, then sniffed her hair, saying, 'Rhoda, this little one should have her face on the cover of those journals I used to like looking at in my youth.' She sighed and added: 'Ruth, child, pay attention to me. Never look vanity in the eye.'

Great-Aunt Minnie dismissed Ruth and clung to Joshua's arm and said, 'Boy, I don't know who you take after.' Then she gave a disapproving sniff and added, 'Boys will be boys.' Joshua got away as soon as he could.

It was my turn now. 'Hope, you are going to be tall and sensible, just like your Great-Grandmother Sadie.' I knew these were words of approval.

'Rhoda.' Great-Aunt Minnie turned to Grandma. 'I hope these children know the history of our family? Children, I was born in 1864, long after abolition.' She swallowed saliva and added, 'Our family did well after slavery was abolished. They acquired this land through blood and sweat; remember that!'

Fresh tears welled up in our eyes when we thought again of all the blood and sweat pouring while our ancestors toiled, backs bent, in the sun. Great-Aunt Minnie told us: 'Your ancestors broke rocks day and night. They sang Negro spirituals, such as "Swing low, sweet chariot, coming for to carry me home", to keep their spirits up.'

Ruth asked politely: 'But Great-Aunt Minnie, if our ancestors were slaves, how did they get this land?'

'Hard work, child,' she answered. 'Hard work!' She asked Uncle Isaiah to pass her the deeds to the land, which she kept in an old brown grip. The papers had turned yellow and were torn in places. Great-Aunt Minnie held the deeds close to her face, peering at the words. She asked each of us to hold the papers. Then she added: 'Our family came from a proud African tribe. We are people who like telling stories.' She had been peering at me as I passed the faded papers to Joshua. 'Hope,' she said, 'you have a wise head and a long way to go. Get a good education and write about your people and the land.'

Great-Aunt Minnie's voice was stern, so I agreed, 'If that's what you want, Great-Aunt Minnie.'

'No, child,' she said seriously. 'It is not what I want. It is what your ancestors would have wanted.'

'I'll do my best,' I half whispered.

'Great-Aunt Minnie,' Joshua asked, accidentally dropping the papers on the floor. 'How can a person's head be wise, and where is Hope going?'

'Joshua.' Great-Aunt Minnie sounded as if she was vexed. '"Labour for learning before you grow old."' She turned to Grandma. 'Rhoda, my senses tell me this boy is as impatient as your father William, who never appreciated that "Learning is better than silver and gold", which will vanish away. Children should be seen and not heard.' Great-Aunt Minnie frowned at Joshua and wagged a finger. 'That is our legacy you've dropped on the floor.

46

Pick it up at once!' She had calmed down now and added: 'Rhoda, I haven't heard you sing in ages. I'd like to hear "By the rivers of Babylon".'

Grandma turned the song into a medley, singing: 'I'm gonna lay down my burden, down by the riverside, down by the riverside...', followed by a chorus of 'In the sweet by and by, we shall meet on that beautiful shore...'

We all tapped our feet and joined in as Great-Aunt Minnie hummed and nodded. Just before she closed her eyes and fell asleep, she said, 'I feel at peace. I've seen the faces of the future generation.' She was carried back to bed by Uncle Isaiah and Aunt Enid who had to stumble about in the darkened room, for Great-Aunt Minnie hated the light.

Grandma rummaged through the old grip. 'Well, look at this,' she said. 'I wasn't bad-looking, if I say so myself.'

We stared at a faded photograph of Grandma and at least a dozen young women: the ladies in the church choir, who were in their early twenties then. They wore long, white dresses and hats. They held song books and were in the act of singing the National Anthem: "Jamaica, Land We Love".

'Grandma! This can't be you,' Ruth exclaimed. 'You look so young and pretty. I thought you were always old.'

Grandma smiled secretly. 'Children,' she said,

'I feel as young as that spring chicken out there on the verandah.'

'But that's a frog,' Joshua said. 'How did it get there and where is that string coming from?' He pointed.

'Prince Charming, Prince Charming!' Ruth cried out when Grandpa appeared. She had read the story of the prince who was turned into a frog, and for a moment her imagination got the better of her. Everyone said Ruth lived in a dream world. She believed everything she read.

Uncle Isaiah and Aunt Enid returned. We went out on to the verandah, where Grandpa held out a plastic frog, attached to a long tube with a small rubber ball on the end. He placed it on the floor and squeezed the ball. The frog's legs inflated and it hopped about.

'I bought it from a higgler on my way here.' Grandpa gave the plastic toy to a smiling Joshua.

Ruth was afraid of frogs and frowned. Grandma said, 'Your grandpa is always playing childish pranks. He's still a boy at heart. We're both as young as ever, even if our hair is grey and we have wrinkles. Anyway, life is like a fairy-story, Ruth. It's good you know so many.'

'Cheer up, Princess Ruth,' Grandpa said. 'I bought this toy frog because I know you are afraid of frogs. You've got to conquer your fear. The countryside is full of frogs.' He began to jig and sing: 'A frog went out on a summer's day, aha, aha. He met Miss Mouse upon the way, aha, aha . . .'

The others joined in, singing: 'Aha, aha, aha, aha . . .' Meantime, my head was full of songs, fairy-stories and the family history. I remembered what Great-Aunt Minnie had said to me. From that moment, I decided that one day I, too, would become a story-teller. I was descended from a long line of story-tellers but I would be the first to put my stories on paper.

6

Sweetie Man

As the months passed school was still a place I dreaded, despite my decision to like it that first night. Ruth had settled in without any problems. Joshua had started now, too, and loved it. The very thought of going to school made me feel ill. I spent many a morning making excuses and thinking of reasons why I couldn't attend. But my grandparents always caught me out, since I was not what they called 'a sickly child'. Whenever we reached the school gate I would be gripped with imaginary tummy ache, toothache, headache or whatever ache came to mind.

'Hope,' Grandma would say, 'remember the boy who cried wolf? One day you will thank me for making sure that you learned to read and write.' Somehow, I seemed to have forgotten that I wanted to write stories.

This dread of school developed because of Precious. Some days she pretended to be nice to me, insisting that I joined her gang. I must say I often did, but that was because I was lonely and desperately wanted to fit in. Everyone seemed so happy in the playground at recess-time. They squabbled occasionally, but their squabbles were short-lived since the girls liked competing with each other, whether they were skipping, dancing or playing jacks.

The boys formed special groups, playing cricket or tossing marbles against walls. Also, whenever a boy got a new toy, the others gathered round and examined it or tried to coax the boy into swapping his toy for a pocketful of marbles or a cricket bat. They rarely succeeded.

One day, the boys gathered round my cousin Robin, who was small and thin. They were trying to get him to swap his harmonica for a pocketful of marbles. But Robin loved playing a tune on his red mouth organ and refused to part with it. No one minded, because Robin was so popular. He was the only boy in our village with a bicycle and the boys knew that he wouldn't let them ride on the handlebars if they were mean to him.

I considered Robin to be my only friend at school because whenever he saw me standing alone in the playground, like a lost sheep, he would desert his friends on the cricket pitch and come to my rescue. Robin's friends grumbled because he was spoiling their game by dropping out, but he ignored them. He told them cousins should keep each other company. We would sit on the grass talking quietly, mainly about Robin's fears. His parents were in England, and he would be joining them shortly. He was terrified of going abroad. He hated the thought of going to a new school and he had nightmares about wandering the length of a newly asphalted playground all alone, with the smell of tar for company.

'You'll make lots of new friends,' I assured him, one day. 'Just you wait and see.'

'But you haven't made any friends here,' Robin said, 'and we are among our own people. I'm going to be an outsider, just like you are now! What if the boys refuse to play with me?' He rose and caught a stray ball. 'And what if . . .' Then a group of boys rushed up to us, they needed an umpire urgently. Robin ran off, declaring, 'I'll only play if I'm the batsman.' Our conversations always ended on an unfinished sentence.

I envied Robin his popularity. It seemed he could do no wrong. Everyone wanted to be his friend, perhaps because they knew that he would be going abroad shortly. They wanted him to send them toys: the boys wanted harmonicas, cricket bats, pocket radios and camping knives, while the girls hoped for cardboard cut-out dolls, hula hoops, jacks sets and skipping ropes.

Many of the younger children thought the streets of London were paved with gold and that everyone was rich. They often said, 'Lucky old Robin Redbreast.' We also thought London Bridge was falling down, and everyone said

London was sinking because it was built on the River Thames.

I had a vivid imagination, so London was a place I cared not to think about too often, because my parents were in London and I thought they would be washed away if the River Thames flooded their house. But that was just a minor worry. My main problem was Precious and her friends: there were Dimples, Zeeta and Pearl, who were cousins. All three girls were skinny with their blue-black skin glistening in the sun. They made my life a misery. They still referred to me as an outsider, discreetly though, and took great pleasure in calling me a 'cry baby'. I cried constantly because all the girls excluded me from their games at recess-time.

Most days I prayed for something terrible to happen to Precious, and today was no exception: Precious had ordered me to turn the skipping rope with another girl while she and her friends skipped and showed off. But she got bored skipping with her friends because they gave in easily, making sure that she won. So she bullied me into skipping with her. The word was passed round that Precious was competing with me. Next thing I noticed was that we were surrounded by a silent crowd.

'Salt, vinegar, mustard, pepper,' Dimples said. 'Pepper, pepper, pepper . . .'

The children formed a wide circle, clapping and chanting along with Dimples. Most of them yelled out Precious's name, because they were afraid of her, though a few rooted for me.

I heard Ruth, Joshua and Robin yelling from afar. Then Robin's friends joined in, followed by some of the girls: 'Faster, faster, Hope!' they shouted in a frenzy.

'Out, out, out . . .' the children chanted when the skipping rope got caught up between Precious's legs. I had won.

'It's all your fault, Zeeta and Pearl!' Precious stormed off in disgrace, and the sound of booing followed her.

That evening Grandma was unable to collect us from school because she was suffering from Hong Kong flu. Robin was with us. Ruth and I giggled over my defeat of Precious. Meantime, Robin's bicycle squeaked along the lonely country lane as Joshua rode on the handlebars.

Precious and her friends were walking ahead of us. 'Cry baby, cry baby . . .' they taunted me. 'You won't be so lucky tomorrow. Just you wait and see.'

'Sticks and stones may break my bones, but words can't harm me . . .' I sang, and the others joined in.

We were so busy out-singing my rivals that we did not see the dust rising in the distance. A black car came round the bend and stopped alongside Precious and her friends.

'Excuse me, children,' said a white man, hanging his head out of the car window. 'Come closer. I'm not going to eat you,' he said, wearing a sly smile. He held out a small paper bag. 'Would anyone like a sweet?'

'Lord, have mercy on us now,' Dimples and Zeeta cried, fleeing in terror. 'Help, help, help . . .' they hollered.

'Run for your life, Precious,' Pearl said, scarpering off.

Precious's skinny legs could be seen scattering as she raced off, shouting: 'Sweetie Man, oh! Sweetie Man, oh!'

The man got out of the car, holding the bag of sweets like bait, saying, 'I only want to know the way to Runaway Bay.'

We had heard stories about Blackheart Men, usually white men who kidnapped black children and cut out their hearts. Now everyone was talking about Sweetie Man, who was said to be a man who tempted children with sweets before kidnapping them.

We children feared for our lives and took flight: Robin abandoned his bicycle and we scrambled over each other as we climbed the stone wall in confusion. We dodged round grazing cattle and sprinted through the pasture, with nettles stinging our legs, not daring to slow down or look back.

'Sweetie Man tried to kidnap us,' Joshua said, flinging himself on the grass outside our home.

'Probably a tourist who strayed off the beaten track,' Grandpa said when we told him the full story. 'I'll go and fetch your bike, Robin,' he said, laughing.

'Honestly!' Robin exclaimed. 'My first glimpse of a foreigner and I behaved like a real country bumpkin.'

'Oh, well.' Grandma sniffed. 'Better safe than sorry.' Then she added: 'Hope, God has answered your prayers at last. I can guarantee you that there will be no more bullying at school from now on. I don't suppose Precious and her friends want anyone to find out how daft they behaved, do you?'

The following day, Precious and her friends pleaded with me not to tell anyone what had happened, and they insisted that I joined their gang. At first I refused, but when I thought of the lonely days ahead, standing in the playground like a lost sheep, I quickly changed my mind.

That afternoon, Precious decided to play a ring game. The players, equal numbers of girls and boys, formed a circle, holding hands. Precious stepped forward. Then the children sang: 'There's a brown girl in the ring, tra la la la la, there's a brown girl in the ring, tra la la la la . . . for she likes sugar and I like plum . . .'

As usual, the singing attracted a large crowd. Most of the children abandoned their games and joined in, forming a wide circle. They chanted: 'Then you skip across the ocean, tra la la la la, then you skip across the ocean, tra la la la la . . . for she likes sugar and I like plum . . .'

The children clapped and sang as Precious skipped across from one side of the ring to the other. They encouraged her to dance, and she wiggled comically until they invited her to 'wheel and take a partner'. She chose me – so did most of the boys and girls. It was as if they were welcoming me to their school at last. Naturally, when it was Robin's turn to choose a partner, he chose me. There were salt-stones on the hillside behind the school and I saw them glistening in the sunlight like diamonds as Robin and I danced to the sound of: 'Then you show me your motion, tra la la la la, then you show me your motion, tra la la la la . . .' I was no longer an outsider.

7

Worshipping Two Masters

On Sundays we attended the village church, which was newly built. It was painted cream with columns supporting a porch. There was a cross on top and louvred windows reflecting in the sun. There were red poinciana trees blooming in the churchyard and the red blossoms littered the grass.

Inside the church, there were holy pictures on the walls, gas lamps hanging from varnished beams, fresh flowers, an altar, pews where the choir sat and a pulpit which was covered with a purple cloth. The wooden floor was polished regularly. As a result, several parishioners had slipped while going up to take communion.

Grandpa wore a suit and tie on Sundays, though he said he felt uncomfortable. Only Joshua rode Gideon, because Ruth and I creased our pastel-coloured chiffon dresses whenever all three of us sat on the horse.

Gideon grazed in the churchyard, along with other horses. We children would go off to Sunday school for an hour while the adults, those that were there to accompany the young children, sat at the back quietly until it was time for the main service. They were making sure we were learning the gospel.

The pastor was a short stout man. He was bald and wore glasses and a grey suit. He rebuked anyone who quarrelled with neighbours, or regularly missed church without a good reason, for the collection plates would be short of change.

'My children,' he announced, after the sinners had repented. 'Let us drink the blood of Christ.'

I fretted because I thought the Communion takers were drinking real blood. One day, I said to Grandpa, 'You must stop Grandma from taking Communion. She is drinking blood.'

Grandpa whispered in my ear, 'Communion is just red wine.'

Grandpa did not take Communion because he said he was a sinner. The pastor had said good Christians did not smoke, drink, dance, worship animals, tell untruths, miss church two weeks in a row or quarrel with their neighbours. Grandpa did not consider himself a good Christian. He drank rum punch often, though he did not smoke. He liked dancing and he worshipped Gideon. He often told small white lies to the pastor, who wanted him to carve statues for his personal collections, free of charge. Occasionally he skipped church in order to avoid the pastor.

Grandma sang in the choir. Many of the congregation would rock and sway as she raised her voice singing 'Rock of Ages, cleft for me'.

There would be a few dissatisfied faces in the congregation, because the elderly parishioners liked to sit in the same place each week. One could hear the sound of a lot of fans snapping shut, Bibles and hymn books being moved along and sharp whispers if they did not have their way.

Almost the whole community turned out on Sundays. People would greet their neighbours: shaking hands and embracing. It was a time to exchange gossip, settle quarrels, admire and coo over new babies, rebuke disobedient teenagers and enquire when courting couples would be getting married.

People would smile down at us and say to our grandparents, 'These children are so well behaved. It will be a sad day when you have to give them up.'

'We'll cross that bridge when we come to it,' Grandpa always said. He hated being reminded that we would be leaving him one day.

Grandma always replied, 'Let us not spoil the Sabbath day with sad thoughts.' Then she would smile tolerantly and add: 'We don't discuss the future in front of the children.'

We, too, hated the thought of leaving our grandparents, because they were more like our real parents now. We thought of our parents often, but they were so far away. We could not imagine them loving us the way our grandparents did.

One Sunday, after Grandma had led the choir in 'O worship the King, all glorious above, O gratefully sing His wonderful love . . .', the pastor preached about loving thy neighbour and forgiving each other. He was rebuking Grandpa because he had quarrelled with a neighbour who owed him money from the sale of Shiloh and Samson. Just then Gideon reared up, neighing at the window, so Grandpa waved at him.

The pastor thumped the pulpit. 'May I remind the congregation that we do not worship animals. We worship God!'

'Amen,' Grandpa said. He then went out to see to Gideon.

Next morning Grandpa was sad, Gideon had died of old age. There was a deep sense of loss as we stared at Gideon's empty trough. Ruth and Joshua clung to Grandpa's legs, weeping, while I stood wondering where Gideon had got the strength to rear and neigh the way he'd done at church.

'A man's best friend is a dog,' Grandma said, trying to cheer up Grandpa. 'We'll get a puppy. You'll soon forget old Gideon.'

The following day, Grandpa buried Gideon near the corral. He said, 'Rhoda, I don't want a puppy-dog. A man's best friend is a horse.' He had planted a rose tree by Gideon's grave. He bowed his head and said reverently, 'Rest in peace, my friend. In time there will be no trace of your grave, but at least the rose tree will be a memorial to you that will last.'

Uncle Isaiah offered to let Grandpa borrow Cheyenne occasionally, but Grandpa refused. He still had Jubal and the mares, though he'd sold the other horses. Man-Man and Big-Man, the hired hands, urged Grandpa to exercise Jubal, but Grandpa said riding Jubal would be like trying to replace Gideon. No. He would not have another pet.

Not long afterwards, Grandma bought a black puppy called Toby. On a cold, misty night, Toby whimpered and crept into the house. We all huddled in the thick cardigans which our parents had sent from England. Grandpa still ignored the puppy until he saw us glaring at him. He sighed and said: 'All right, but he's not allowed to sleep in the house in future. I'll have to make him a kennel.'

After that, Grandpa was besotted with Toby. The puppy followed him everywhere. One particular Sunday, we were in church. The floor was highly polished as usual and we smelled the beeswax as we listened to the pastor, saying: 'Brothers and sisters, seek, and you shall find. Ask, and it will be given. Knock, and the door will open!'

There was a loud tapping outside the church door, which was open. The congregation cleared their throats to stifle giggles when they saw Toby running down the aisle, sniffing and looking for Grandpa. He barked loudly when he found him.

The pastor thumped the pulpit: 'My children, you cannot worship two masters!'

'Amen,' Grandpa agreed.

We made room for Toby. He sat quietly listening to the pastor. But when Grandma led the choir, Toby recognized her voice and began to bark. Grandma was singing 'Stand up! Stand up for Jesus! Ye soldiers of the cross . . .' For the first time in fifty years she was lost for words and just stood there with her mouth open.

'Brother Noah.' The pastor came down from the pulpit. 'I have nothing against animals, but I do not want them in my house.' Then he slipped and fell on the polished floor, muttering.

'Ahem.' Grandma cleared her throat.

Grandpa went to help the pastor. 'It seems God is reminding you that this is his house after all, Pastor.'

No one could suppress the giggling now as hymn books fell to the floor. Then the congregation said: 'Praise the Lord! Never a truer word said, brother Noah!'

8

The Journey

Grandma had not seen her brother Lincoln, our great-uncle, for a long time, so she promised to take Robin and me to visit him. Robin's grandma, Great-Aunt Esmé, could not make the journey, for her bunions were playing up. Robin's grandfather, Great-Uncle Ely, brought him down to our cottage, early one morning. Great-Uncle Ely was a small man, whose tummy hung over his trousers. He waved Robin off then he returned home. He had a farm to run and the animals had not been fed.

Grandpa and Toby stood by the gate. He placed my water container round my neck and a basket on Grandma's head. She was holding a cutlass. Then Grandpa waved us off, with Toby barking, and Ruth and Joshua stood on the verandah with puffed-up faces; they both had mumps. They desperately wanted to come with us and somehow their faces looked exceptionally bloated.

'Never mind, Ruth and Joshua,' Grandpa said. 'I'll give you a piggy-back round the farm later. That'll cheer you up.'

Robin carried a billy can and his red

harmonica. He wore denims and a striped shirt. Grandma wore her red headscarf and a red dress while I wore blue dungarees. We were all wearing gum boots.

We passed fields where okras were being harvested. Then we saw trees bearing white, sweet-smelling shoots, shaped like trumpets. I asked Grandma why the grass flattened under our feet as we walked.

'This is chameleon grass,' Grandma said. 'It flattens when it is disturbed.'

We greeted the farmers who gave us okras, which we placed in Grandma's basket before starting the journey uphill. Along the way, we heard grunting and Grandma pointed to a tree and shouted: 'Wild boars, children. Quick, quick, let's climb that tree.'

The basket fell from Grandma's head, but she held on to the cutlass. Robin dropped the billy can as we climbed the tree. We managed to find a perch and sat looking down at the boars. One of them had got the billy can stuck on its snout. It spun around in a fury, grunting until the can fell off.

The slender pimento tree wavered under our weight as we clung to the limbs, while Grandma decided what to do. She decided to chop a branch down with her cutlass. Tiny grains of pimentos rained down on the boars. They grunted and fled into the high ferns, sending stones rolling down the hillside.

It was now safe to climb down.

'Children, take a good look at this place. You will never see it again,' Grandma said before she helped us down from the tree and picked up the basket and the billy can.

Robin and I took in trembling bamboo trees, butterflies, wild fowls and snails and lizards of different sizes, crawling on the ground. The scent of pawpaws, ginger, pimentos and wild flowers lingered as avocados glistened in the sunlight.

'One day I'll come back to this place,' Robin said firmly.

'I doubt it,' Grandma said. 'When people go to foreign, they tend to forget where they are coming from.'

'You're wrong, Grandma,' I said. 'I'll never forget where I'm coming from, and I don't want to go to England: I can't bear the thought of leaving you and Grandpa, going to a new school and becoming an outsider again!'

'You're a born worrier, Hope,' Grandma said. 'Come along. Let's not spoil our adventure with sad thoughts.'

'Quite right.' Robin began to play 'She'll be coming round the mountain when she comes . . .'

We reached the top of the hill and a frightened rabbit slid past. To our amazement Grandma announced: 'Children, let's make this a real adventure and slide down on our bottoms.'

A huge silver bird flew high above and I realized that it was an aeroplane. But I soon began to laugh at what was happening on earth. An old woman with a basket on her head and two children behind, holding each other around the waist, slowly slid down the hillside, with the billy can and the cutlass reflecting in the sun, sending rays shimmering in the distance. We all laughed and laughed as we bumped our way down.

We arrived at a river where we saw a rainbow and the colours reflected in the water.

'Always make a wish when you see a rainbow, children,' Grandma said, filling the billy can. She pointed across the river. 'There's your Great-Uncle Lincoln's cottage.'

My wish was to stay with Grandma for ever, but of course I had no idea what Robin had wished for. I knew you mustn't ever say your wish out loud. It won't come true if you do.

We approached a small cottage with lots of pink roses. Whitewashed stones lined the path and a mangy dog stood by the verandah, growling at us.

Great-Uncle Lincoln stooped and came out from a smoke-filled kitchen. He had coffee-coloured skin and his grey eyes were cat-like. His wife had died long ago and his children were in America, so he lived alone. He was a retired tailor, but he was kept busy because the elderly villagers preferred homemade clothes as ready-made clothes were not so hardwearing.

'Children,' Great-Uncle Lincoln greeted us as he embraced us. 'You're just in time for supper.' The scent of smoke and fish lingered on his clothes. The dog growled so Great-Uncle Lincoln told him: 'Ah, Prince, stop moaning and be quiet.'

Prince whimpered and settled down, lying across the doorway as if he wanted to keep us out of the sitting-room. We stayed on the verandah. Grandma insisted on taking over in the kitchen. Great-Uncle Lincoln agreed, pleased to have a meal served by someone else. He decided to continue with his work. Robin and I sat on the verandah watching him as he pedalled his Singer sewing machine. He was making a pair of trousers. He was an old man with very bony kneecaps, but he pedalled that sewing machine like a young man.

At suppertime, we had fried fish and Johnny cakes on the verandah while insects buzzed around the kerosene lamp. Great-Uncle Lincoln told us more about the family history. He said, 'Children, one of our ancestors was the son of an English planter. He fell in love with a Negress, called Kalinda. But he was shipped off to England, unaware that Kalinda was with child. She gave birth to twins: Great-

Grandmother Sadie and Great-Aunt Lilian, whose looks Ruth has inherited.' He drew breath then continued. 'Great-Grandmother Sadie married your Great-Aunt Minnie's eldest brother, Manroot. He carried himself as proud and tall as a king, even in old age. He was also a great story-teller.'

Next day, we hugged Great-Uncle Lincoln. We took the main road home. We never saw Great-Uncle Lincoln again. But I never forgot him: peace and love radiated from his face, and I felt privileged to have known him.

On the way home, we passed several signposts, one leading to the village of York Castle. Then we approached our village and stopped to look at an old ruin named Edinburgh Castle.

'I thought they only had castles in England,' Robin said.

Grandma put down the basket. 'When the English captured Jamaica from the Spaniards, they built forts and gave them English names.' She pointed. 'Children, this castle was once owned by Lewis Hutchinson, a madman who kidnapped travellers and killed them during the days of slavery. He used to throw the bodies down a sinkhole, not far from here, called 'Hutchinson's Hole'. He was hanged for his crimes in Spanish Town. I believe there is a book called *Tales of Old Jamaica*, which tells the story of Hutchinson and other famous

Jamaicans of his time.' She picked up the basket.

'I didn't know you knew about real history, Aunt Rhoda!' Robin exclaimed. 'I thought you only knew Anancy-stories.'

'You live and learn, Robin,' Grandma chuckled.

Late that evening, Robin's grandparents collected him, saying, 'You have another journey ahead of you, young man. You are going to your parents in England.'

That Sunday, Robin went up to the altar where the pastor blessed him, saying: 'When in Rome you do as the Romans do, but never forget your past.' He presented him with a Bible.

After the service was over, Robin stood under one of the red poinciana trees in the churchyard. His grandparents stood behind him. They smiled as he shook hands with all the churchgoers who were crying and reminding him to write.

'I wonder if the streets of London are really paved with gold?' Robin asked.

I did not reply, because I thought all the gold was in a country called El Dorado. I stared at Robin, who held a cap in his hand and was perspiring in a thick black suit. He reminded me of a little man.

'It will be your turn next,' Robin whispered in my ear. Then he burst into tears. I thought he was crying because he did not want to leave the village. Instead he said, 'I lost my mouth organ yesterday. What will I do without it? Suppose they don't have mouth organs in England?'

'They do,' Grandma said. 'And you'd better get used to calling it a harmonica.'

I was angry with Robin for reminding me that I, too, would be going to England one day. I snapped at him, saying, 'I'm glad you lost your silly, old mouth organ.' I clung to Grandma and refused to say goodbye to Robin.

'Hope,' Grandma said, pulling me away, 'that is no way to part with your cousin. Shake hands with Robin now.'

I sniffed, held out my hand and said in an adult tone, 'Till we meet again, Robin.'

Just then, my heart missed a beat because I longed to see my parents. Then I remembered the photograph they had recently sent us and I promised myself to look at it later.

Parting with Robin was very sad. I had never realized how much I valued his friendship. I was beginning to miss him already, but I said to myself, 'Absence makes the heart grow fonder.'

9

Christmas Time Is Coming Soon

Christmas was a long time coming when we children were growing up. We were impatient for December to come round and regularly checked Grandpa's almanac. I can still recall the first time we went to Christmas market with Grandma. It was a grand occasion.

At dawn, we boarded the country bus, heading for Kingston. I clearly remember the cocks crowing: 'Cock-a-doodle-do, cock-a-doodle-do.' The bus swerved several times as it climbed the winding hill, but none of the other passengers paid any attention; they kept dozing off.

At last we arrived and filed off the bus. Then we caught sight of hundreds of coloured light bulbs, blinking along the main road. There was no electricity in our village, so the flashing lights were a sight to behold.

The scent of roasted coffee beans and fried fish came from a nearby shop, bearing the sign 'Auntie Lulu's Diner'. But we didn't go there. We followed Grandma into the market-place, where the higglers were already selling their wares.

Grandma stopped at a stall and admired the delicate pastel chiffon, satin and sequinned materials. Meanwhile, we children stared at Christmas decorations, balloons, coloured streamers and anything that appeared bright and shiny.

A few of the higglers knew Grandma. They embraced her, saying, 'Rhoda, dis long time gal me never see yuh.' The happy-go-lucky bunch were noisy and colourful. They cackled: 'Children, when yuh go to foreign, tell your parents that Mama Elvira, Aunti Flora and Cousin Vashti said to say howdy-do.'

'Rhoda, gal,' said a woman standing behind us, 'my gran'children gone a foreign, dear. I jus' got one of those pretty-pretty, snow-covered Christmas cards from dem.'

'How's life treating you, Auntie Lulu?' Grandma said.

Aunti Lulu was a big woman, wearing a plaid dress and a large straw hat. She held a wicker basket and her fat chin wobbled as she said: 'Ah, chile, I'm bearing up, me dear. Yuh wait till it's your turn to part with these pickneys.'

Grandma hated such discussions. She bought fresh fish and promised to spend the afternoon with Auntie Lulu, catching up on old times. We moved on, stopping at a stall where we admired a variety of toys: there were wooden tops, jacks sets, yo-yos, hula hoops, aeroplanes and harmonicas.

An old man sat on a stool near by, playing a concertina and singing: 'You better watch out, you better watch out, Santa Claus is coming to town . . .'

'Who's Santa Claus?' asked Joshua.

'Father Christmas, of course,' Ruth exclaimed.

We stopped at the next stall, where Grandma bought three helium balloons, bright coloured whistles and shiny, pyramid-shaped Christmas hats with crepe streamers flying upwards. We walked in the morning sun, blowing our whistles and feeling as if our faces would burst with happiness.

The market-place was full of laughter and music. Then the string of my balloon worked its way loose and I felt as if happiness had been snatched away from me. Meantime, the old man continued playing his concertina and singing: 'Jolly old St Nicholas, lean your ears this way, don't you tell a single soul what I'm going to say, Christmas time is coming soon . . .'

'Never mind,' Grandma said. 'Maybe Santa Claus will bring you something special. Go on, make a wish.'

I closed my eyes, wishing to see my parents. But I opened them when I heard a commotion. Children stood on tip-toe, pushing and shoving to get a better view. We saw people dressed in flamboyant red devil costumes, carrying pitchforks and swaying to the beat of drums.

There were also bands of young people wearing gay, colourful clothes and a few wore horses' heads face masks.

'Why are people in fancy dress, Grandma?' Joshua asked.

'They are celebrating Jonkonnu,' Grandma said. 'It's rare nowadays, but in the past our people had little time for celebrations, so during the Christmas and New Year holidays they dressed in fancy costumes and masqueraded in the streets.'

'I wish Mother and Father were here now,' Ruth said. 'They're missing all the fun.'

The commotion made conversation impossible!

'Jonkonnu, Jonkonnu,' the children clapped and shouted when a man wearing a horse's head approached us, dancing the calypso. I became so excited I forgot about my balloon. We followed the man wearing the horse's head as though he was the Pied Piper of Hamlyn. 'Jonkonnu, Jonkonnu,' we continued shouting and many parents had trouble keeping up with their children, who acted as if they'd fallen under a spell.

Grandma was relieved when Ruth and Joshua said they were hungry. We retired to 'Auntie Lulu's Diner', where we ate rice 'n' peas and chicken for lunch. We listened to Christmas carols blaring out over the wireless. Strangers hugged each other and bought aerated water for one and all, shaking hands and saying 'Happy Christmas' until sunset arrived. Suddenly, the sky lit up and we stood outside the shop, spellbound, watching a real firework display.

On Christmas Day we went to church early, because the Sunday school children were going to perform the nativity play. Parents sat proudly, nodding and saying in their strict voices: 'Speak up, children. We can't hear you at the back.'

There were many sad faces as Mary, Joseph and the donkey were turned away from the inn. But they cheered up when Mary and Joseph finally found a stable. Next the three wise men arrived, bearing gifts of gold, frankincense and myrrh for the new-born King, and make-believe stars twinkled in the church.

The children recited: 'And he sent them to Bethlehem and said, "Go and search diligently for the young child . . ."' Then we sang: 'Little donkey, little donkey, had a heavy load . . .'

'Eeh, aah, eeh, aah, eeh, aah . . .' The sound of braying came from outside the church. We children stood before the congregation, biting our lips and trying not to giggle. One of the parishioners left his seat, bowing his head, ashamed, for it was his donkey that was braying in the churchyard.

'Alleluia! Praise the Lord! Amen!' The deacons said, pretending nothing had happened. The organ sounded and the congregation began to sing: 'O come, all ye faithful, joyful and triumphant, O come ye, O come ye to Bethlehem . . .'

We children silently returned to our seats, having played the parts of shepherds pointing to a star in the east. Then the pastor preached a sermon about peace and goodwill to all, at home and abroad. He had recently returned from a Baptist convention in America, where he had studied theology in his youth. He wished everyone a Merry Christmas, adding: 'When I was in America, I used to love this Christmas carol.' He led the choir into singing 'I'm Dreaming of a White Christmas'.

'I wonder what a white Christmas looks like?' Joshua asked.

'Me too,' Ruth said.

'Umh,' I muttered. I wondered too as I thought of the Christmas card that we had received from our parents: Father Christmas stood by a cast-iron fireplace, holding a red sack and looking very jolly.

Grandpa stopped singing and said seriously: 'Children, let us make the most of our green, sunny Christmas and leave white Christmas to the future.'

10

Waiting for the Harvest

Our village consisted of small farms and one large cattle ranch, which was owned by a man called Mas Busha. He was a quadroon and a fourth generation of ranchers. Often we had to climb on to the top of the stone walls when Mas Busha and his hired hands went on a cattle drive, moving the herd to new pastures, because there were many fierce bulls and they stampeded down the lanes, mooing and butting everything in sight. Mas Busha had to divert the cattle away from the village square. But unfortunately some of the small farms nearest the village were affected, because often the cattle strayed on to the farmers' land, trampling their crops.

Uncle Isaiah's field was miles away from the village, so his crop was spared the assault. We children never forgot the incident with the mouse, but somehow we were always drawn back to Uncle Isaiah's field. We still marvelled at the endless rows of corn and hundreds of chattering parakeets.

Harvest time was approaching and Uncle Isaiah was unpopular with the other farmers, because, although the cattle had not stampeded their fields this season, their crops were blighted while his crop thrived. He was 'born lucky'. The farmers said our family had got the best land after abolition and because Uncle Isaiah's field stood on an underground river, the land was irrigated. We children would lie on our stomachs, ears to the ground, listening in vain for the sound of running water.

It was the month of March and the scarecrows and ground doves were plentiful. The doves boldly perched on the scarecrows' straw hats and wooden arms, cooing until we chased them off. Meantime, Uncle Isaiah guarded his record crop from the parakeets by knocking empty kerosene-pans in order to scare them off. He did not have a gun, because law-abiding citizens did not carry firearms.

The farmers stopped by Uncle Isaiah's field frequently, blaming Mas Busha and his cattle for ruining their crops. But everyone knew that most of the cattle had been shipped off to America, and there hadn't been a cattle drive in ages. No. The farmers neglected their land, unlike Uncle Isaiah who tilled the soil and fertilized the land often.

One day, Mas Busha reined in his horse, saying, 'Isaiah, yuh crop doin' well, man. Looks like yuh 'ave green fingas. Dat's wat I keep telling dese farmers.'

We children stared at Uncle Isaiah's long dark

fingers. There was nothing green about them.

'Uncle Isaiah,' Joshua asked, 'what is Mas Busha saying? Your fingers aren't green.'

Uncle Isaiah took in Mas Busha's weather-beaten face. 'Children, I have planters' hands, unlike some people.'

Mas Busha's real name was Joseph, but everyone called him 'Busha' because he owned a lot of land. He had never chopped wood or tilled the soil in his entire life. He had inherited a large property from his father, to be passed on to his daughter, Miss Girlie, who had married an American artist. The farmers resented Mas Busha, who sat on his verandah reading his newspaper like a lord, while they trudged home wearily after a hard day toiling in the sun. Everyone said the only good thing about Mas Busha was that he spoke in 'raw patois'.

Mas Busha rode off, saying: 'Isaiah, yuh speaking in riddles, man. Tell de pickneys wat green fingas is!'

Uncle Isaiah said, 'Children, the term "green fingers" is a mystery to me. All I know is that whatever I plant it grows, regardless of whether I till the soil or fertilize the land.'

We stopped for lunch and Joshua said, 'Uncle Isaiah, you haven't set any traps, have you?'

Uncle Isaiah had roasted corn on the cob for lunch. He handed us each a corn cob. 'Joshua,' he said, 'whatever happened to that angry little boy who wanted to learn how to set traps to kill animals? Surely you haven't forgotten what happened to your grandma's favourite hen, Frizzle?'

'I'll never forget that day,' Ruth said sadly.

'Me neither,' Joshua said. 'But I can't stand the way the poor animals struggle when they're caught, not to mention the whimpering and squeaking. I have to release them.'

Uncle Isaiah shook his head, smiling. 'You children would beg mercy for a fly,' he said: 'Oh, well, "Blessed are the merciful, for they shall obtain mercy".'

'Don't worry, Uncle Isaiah,' I said, savouring the corn. 'We haven't forgotten the incident, but we've forgiven you.'

We finished our lunch in silence. Then Uncle Isaiah added, 'Let's go and join the workers, children.'

There were at least a dozen men in the field: Some swung scythes and machetes while others kept their distance from the sharp instruments, bagging the corn in hessian sacks. They began to sing a folk song:

'Sammy plant piece a corn dung a gully, mm
An' it bear till it kill poor Sammy, mm
 Sammy dead, Sammy dead, Sammy dead oh! mm
 Sammy dead, Sammy dead, Sammy dead oh! mm
A no tief Sammy tief mek dem kill him, mm
A no lie Sammy lie mek him dead oh! mm

But a grudgeful dem grudgeful kill Sammy,
mm

But a grudgeful dem grudgeful kill Sammy,
mm

Neighbour cyan bear fe see neighbour
flourish, mm

Neighbour cyan bear fe see neighbour
flourish, mm

Sammy dead, Sammy dead, Sammy dead
oh! mm

Sammy dead, Sammy dead, Sammy dead
oh! mm

Sammy gone dung a hell fe shoot blackbud,
mm

A no lie Sammy lie mek him go deh, mm

But a grudgeful dem grudgeful kill Sammy,
mm

Sammy dead, Sammy dead, Sammy dead oh!
mm . . .'

The lead singer was called One-Eyed Jack. He was a white-haired old man with a patch over his left eye. He stopped singing while the others hummed: 'mm, mm . . .' Then he said, 'Mas Isaiah, yuh in de fiel' from sun-up till sun-dung. Mind yuh nuh work yourself into de groun' like poor old Sammy, mm!'

The men put down their tools and Uncle Isaiah said: 'Hard work never harmed a man; back to work, boys.'

One-Eyed Jack said, 'Mas Isaiah, slavery was

abolished in eighteen-sinting. Yuh cyan keep working de men dem like slaves. Do eberyting in moderation, sah!'

We instantly saw Uncle Isaiah as a hard taskmaster. He had upset us again. Suddenly the rows of corn, the scarecrows and the chattering parakeets were no longer appealing.

'Boys,' Uncle Isaiah said, 'when the harvesting is over, we'll have a drink in the rum bar, all right?'

'Dat's more like it,' One-Eyed Jack said.

We children were in awe of One-Eyed Jack, who was clearly rebuking Uncle Isaiah. He and the men picked up their tools and went off, singing another folk song:

'Day oh, day oh,
Day da light an' me wan' go home.
Day oh, day oh,
Day da light an' me wan' go home.
Come Missa Tallyman come tally me banana,
Day da light an' me wan' go home.
Come fix yu catta, Matty, fe come tek bunch
    banana,
Day da light an' me wan' go home.
Me come yah fe work, me no come yah fe
    idle . . .
Day da light an' me wan' go home.
No gimme so so bunch me no horse wid
    bridle . . .
Day da light an' me wan' go home . . .'

Harvest Sunday arrived. Some of the parishioners brought along livestock instead of food. Several chickens, with their legs tied, were soon hopping around the churchyard. The church was full of flowers. There was an abundance of fruit and vegetables at the altar waiting to be blessed. The younger children stood up front, clutching their baskets of eggs and fruit while one boy carried a rooster under his arm and looked rather uncomfortable. They all waited to be blessed.

The pastor preached about the generosity of his flock. Then he recited: 'Though I bestow all my goods to feed the poor . . . and have not charity, it profiteth me nothing.'

'Praise the Lord!' The congregation nodded.

Uncle Isaiah and Aunt Enid sat erect, smiling. We were very proud of him for his generosity. He had donated half of his harvest to the church bazaar, which was to be held on the following day. The proceeds, along with food parcels, would be distributed to the needy afterwards. Uncle Isaiah's bumper crop was recorded in the parish register. A lot of people were envious, not only of the crop but because the pastor had personally congratulated Uncle Isaiah before the service had begun.

The choir sang: 'We plough the fields, and scatter the good seed on the land; But it is fed and watered by God's almighty hands . . .' Then the rooster crowed, startling everyone.

One-Eyed Jack had been dozing. He opened his eye, saying: 'Cock crowing, cock crowing, mus' be daylight!' He hissed through his teeth in order to conceal his embarrassment. Then he added: 'Mm, Cock crowin' in chapel, dis mus' be a sign, breddas!'

Mas Busha was sitting behind Uncle Isaiah. He patted him on the back, saying, 'Yes, sah! De cock's crowin' on Isaiah's behalf.' He clasped Uncle Isaiah's hand. 'Gimme five, man. Yuh mus' be feelin' as proud as a peacock right now!'

A few people rose and shook Uncle Isaiah's hand. Then the choir sang: 'Sowing in the morning, sowing seeds of kindness . . . waiting for the harvest, and the time of reaping, we shall come rejoicing, bringing in the sheaves . . .'

'Brothers and sisters,' the pastor said, 'you reap according to what you sow: make hay while the sun shines and you can all look forward to record crops next year!'

'Mm,' the congregation grudgingly agreed.

11

Festival Time

It was 5 August and the villagers were excited. Everyone was looking forward to the following day, which was another Independence Day celebration.* They spent the whole week whitewashing their cottages and the stones that led up the paths.

Grandma had made sorrel wine, coconut cakes, corn-pone and our favourite biscuits which were shaped like animals. There was also plenty of aerated water to drink, because we were going to have a picnic on the village green.

Our cottage was situated near the crossroads, and that evening many people stopped at our gate, discussing the progress Jamaica had made since 1962, though I never understood the importance of the date.

I looked into the sitting-room, where a white tablecloth trembled in the night air. Grandma had embroidered Happy Independence Day in green, black and gold letters around the hem. There was a bowl of fruit on the table, and we sniffed the scent of pineapples, which was the fruit engraved on the Jamaica coat of arms.

* Jamaica had gained her independence from England in 1962

We children were allowed to stay up late. We listened to the radio, broadcasting festival songs, and the people in Kingston sending greetings to Jamaicans all over the world. At that time, Kingston seemed far away as we quietly listened to the voices coming at us, while the fireworks boomed out over the air waves.

Man-Man and Big-Man, the hired hands, were passing the time with us. They had earlier hitched up their horses by the gate. We children stared at the men. They both wore gold watches and leather boots, which they had bought in America. And I decided America was the richest country in the world. I hummed, 'I want to be in America.'

'I hope the pastor isn't going to spend all day tomorrow singing Gospel songs and the national anthem,' Big-Man said.

'Let's make sure he doesn't,' Man-Man said. Then he drawled, 'Jamaica is moving up in the world. Time we were getting in the groove.' I thought he would burst into song any minute because he had such a musical-sounding voice.

Grandma and Grandpa shelled Jerusalem beans and the beans fell into a large, white enamel bowl, one after the other: ping, pong, ping, pong, while the people in Kingston continued sending messages over the radio. We children were on best behaviour because we were so pleased to be staying up late; we remained silent and listened to the radio.

'Progress is coming to Jamaica,' Man-Man said. 'We are exporting our goods, and there's also tourism. The Americans flock here like those white gulls down by the corral. Yes, man, we'll soon be a rich nation.' He caught a firefly and watched the insect crawling up his arm. When it reached his shoulder, with its light flickering on and off, he rose and yawned, saying, 'What I hate about country life is the lack of electricity. But thank God, we've got a full moon tonight. We'd better get going. We've got big plans for tomorrow.'

The horses' hooves echoed along the road as the moon came up on the horizon. The village drunk, Taa-Ta, arrived. He was a tall yellow-skinned man, who reeked of rum. He wore a faded shirt and trousers held up with a piece of string. He chewed on his gum as he said good evening, and pulled up a chair.

'Evening, Taa-Ta,' Grandma and Grandpa said at once. 'We don't often get the pleasure of your company.'

'Me givin' de rum bar a miss,' Taa-Ta said, as though he was convincing himself. He addressed us, saying, 'Children, we free of Colonial rule now. Everyone should get drunk an' celebrate de sixth of August in style, dancin' an' singin' all de festival songs dat 'ave come an' gone since we've become independent of De Maddah Country. Yes, sir-ee,' he hiccupped.

'I don't think the pastor would be pleased if

he heard you saying that,' Grandpa chuckled. 'You know how he feels about music and dancing.'

'No doubt he'll be praisin' de Lard an' calling down de angels tomorrow,' Taa-Ta said, sighing.

The country bus sounded its horn in the distance, getting louder and louder. The passengers, mainly higglers returning from the market in Kingston, sang the national song to the tune of 'I Vow to Thee my Country'. The sound of 'O green isle of the Indies, Jamaica, strong and free' came at us as the voices got nearer. Then they started at the beginning, singing: 'I pledge my heart for ever, to serve with humble pride . . .'

The moon hung in the sky like a ball filled with water. Grandpa stared at it, saying, 'Every year the same thing happens: people sing and pray, but Jamaica is still poor. It seems we have a long way to go.'

'Amen,' Grandma said. 'Let us pray for the prosperity of our nation.'

'No doubt we'll be doin' a lot of dat tomorrow,' Taa-Ta said, rising.

The following afternoon, we picnicked on the village green: firecrackers were set off, sailing into the sky along with balloons, while children waved tiny Jamaican flags. The women in the church choir sang one song after another, ending with 'Jamaica, Jamaica, Jamaica, land we love'. Then we all recited the national pledge: 'Before God and all mankind, I pledge my love, my loyalty and skills in the service of Jamaica and my fellow citizens . . .'

The children soon became restless and many adults were tired of, what Grandpa called, 'the show of nationalism'. Meantime, the elderly villagers, who were placed in the shade, sat in their chairs, being fanned by relatives. A few dozed off, snoring with their mouths open, while others squinted in the sunlight, complaining that too much merrymaking was bad for the soul.

Many stalls and booths were erected, and the higglers sold their wares, laughing and competing with each other. Different activities were laid on for the children: there was the egg and spoon race, the potato-sack race, the relay and the tug-o-war. The adults cheered the children on, but we children were too shy to take part. We stayed close to our grandparents, happy to observe from afar. Then someone shouted that it was time for parents to join in, and Grandpa was first in line.

'Go, Grandpa, go,' we yelled, becoming brave.

'You can do it, Grandpa,' Ruth yelled. 'You've got much longer legs than anyone else.'

The funniest thing about Grandpa was that he was the tallest person present. The hessian sack he was hopping about in barely passed his kneecaps, but that did not stop him from enjoying himself. Then Grandma entered the egg and spoon race. Her white pleated dress fanned around her as the sun reflected on her glasses. She and Grandpa did not win any prizes, but we were proud of them for trying.

'Brother Noah and sister Rhoda.' The pastor approached, frowning. 'Fancy you two forgetting your age.'

'Well, Pastor,' Grandpa said, catching his breath, 'even Christians are allowed to enjoy themselves occasionally.'

Just then we heard raised voices and the sound of drums: 'Boom, back a boom, back a boom, back a boom . . .'

'Brothers and sisters,' the pastor said, raising his hands in horror, 'this is a day of thanksgiving. Do not dance to the devil's tune! Let us pray for the sinners.'

But Grandpa was already doing a jig. He spun Grandma around and said, 'Pastor, man cannot live on prayers alone.'

Man-Man and Big-Man approached, beating the drums. They were dressed in denims and plaid shirts. They began to sing: 'Move up, now, Jamaica, move up. Jamaica now is on the move. All are getting in the groove. Out of many, we are one . . .'

'Yes, man,' a voice shouted. 'Shake a leg, Pastor.' It was the village drunk, Taa-Ta. He staggered into the crowd smelling of rum. We children were wide-eyed with excitement as we huddled together, giggling. Taa-Ta was dressed in a floral shirt, cut-down khaki trousers and the brim of an old straw hat. He was wearing shoes, but no socks. His legs were thin and hairy. He poised himself and dragged his words, saying: 'People, get ready, let's do de rock steady. It's baa-baa, boom time!'

'Well,' the pastor huffed. 'This is outrageous.'

'Cho! Pastor.' Mas Busha approached. 'Dere's a time an' place fe everything. Stop mek-mekin' an' enjoy yourself, man!'

The pastor was outnumbered. He gave up and joined the elderly parishioners. By now dusk was approaching. The grass on the village green flattened as Man-Man and Big-Man beat the drums, and Taa-Ta encouraged everyone to join in. Adults and children danced the rock steady and sang: 'Baa-baa boom, festival, baa-baa boom, festival . . .'

Now we children forgot our shyness and joined in the jamboree, dancing the rock steady until we were exhausted. The scent of curried mutton 'n' rice was carried on the breeze, and the villagers decided it was time to rest their legs. They sat on the grass eating, discussing politics or telling folk tales.

'Dat's de trouble wid yuh folks,' declared one of the villagers, Papa Zack, who was a widower. 'Always livin' in de past and worshippin' politicians.'

'Yuh right, Papa Zack!' Taa-Ta shouted. ''Ere's to de future!' He staggered off with a rum bottle in his hand.

'No point in pledgin' yuh 'eart an' promisin' fe love Jamaica if de government no doin' anythin' fe improve we life,' Papa Zack snapped. 'Jus' think! everybody in 'Merica 'ave runnin' wata an' electricity, an' dem pickneys get de best education money can buy. Wat sort a future your pickneys dem gwine 'ave, tell me dat?'

Papa Zack's only child was called Son-Son. He was sixteen years old and built like a bean pole. He was a clever boy, but his father could not afford to further his education. Everyone said it was 'a crying shame', for Son-Son's brain was 'like an adding machine', but no one had the means to help him.

The merrymaking ended. No one spoke, but I sensed that they all agreed with Papa Zack, who was a dark man with an unsmiling face and a habit of chewing tobacco. I realized then that we children were lucky: we had a future to look forward to, unlike Son-Son. I also understood Papa Zack's lack of patriotism. After all, we were now a free nation, so what were the politicians doing to improve our country? I vowed then never to celebrate another Independence Day, not unless Jamaica had really prospered.

12

The Storm

Time passed and Great-Aunt Minnie died. We children were sad, but Grandma said Great-Aunt Minnie's spirit was at peace now. We helped on Grandpa's farm. Ruth and Joshua fed the chickens. Grandpa looked after the horses. He also chopped firewood and kept the grass low, while I helped Grandma with the pigs.

Aunt Esmé and Uncle Ely visited us often, for they were lonely now that Robin had gone. They were so proud of Robin, who had settled in school. They sat on the verandah and told us how he had turned into a real English boy, because they needed a dictionary to understand half of the words in his letters!

One Saturday evening, Joshua sat listening to the conversation and suddenly said: 'Aunt Esmé, Uncle Ely, I don't see why you keep worrying about Robin. After all, he's only moved to Kingston. That's where Mother and Father live.'

'They've probably forgotten us,' Ruth said sadly. 'Besides, I can't even remember them. This photograph doesn't look like Father.' She stared at the photo of a tall man, wearing a suit that was different from Father's.

I myself stared at a tall, slender woman in a blue chiffon dress standing next to Father. They were both smiling. I had looked at the photograph again and again, but now for the first time I realized that Father did look different. Perhaps because the smile never moved. It was as if I only vaguely remembered him and Mother. It was now three years since they had gone. Mother seemed so much thinner and more serious.

Aunt Esmé wore a string of glass beads, which twinkled around her neck. She ignored Joshua's remark and sat massaging her bunions, saying: 'Rhoda, children are not like old people; they can adjust to any situation.'

Grandpa held a glass of rum punch. It was a long time since he'd danced his little jig. He finished the punch and stared above the hillside, saying, 'Storm clouds are gathering. I'd better see to the animals.'

The clouds had been gathering for days. It was just Grandpa's way of getting away from Aunt Esmé and Uncle Ely. He hated being reminded that we, too, would leave him one day.

Later that night, Aunt Enid came down to our cottage. She was wearing her blue dress and gingham apron as usual, but her thin face drooped and her chin touched her chest as she sat in Grandma's rocking-chair weeping and saying, 'Something has happened to Isaiah down at the field.'

I handed her a glass of water. Her hand was clammy as she touched my arm and thanked me. Then I said, 'Don't worry, Aunt Enid. God will protect him.'

'Let's hope so,' she said wearily.

Grandpa went to fetch Uncle Ely and then they rode to Uncle Isaiah's field. It was dawn when they returned. Uncle Isaiah was being carried on a litter, drawn by Cheyenne. The horse was foaming at the mouth and his eyes rolled in confusion.

'Oh, no!' I moaned. My legs trembled as the dew glistened on the grass, while Cheyenne neighed and stamped his hooves. It was really frightening. The horse would not let anyone, except Grandpa, near Uncle Isaiah, not even Aunt Enid.

Uncle Isaiah had had a massive stroke. We children walked around on tiptoe whenever we visited. Grandma said we had to keep up the vigil, because if we talked to Uncle Isaiah he would get better. But day by day, he slipped away from us.

The rain never stopped falling. Grandpa said Uncle Isaiah's spirit was low. He could only blink his eyelids and could hardly open his twisted lips. Then one evening after Grandma had bathed Uncle Isaiah and fed him his favourite spinach soup, Aunt Enid took over the shift. Suddenly, she hollered and passers-by came running. She told them: 'Isaiah has crossed the River Jordan!'

Two days later, we filed in to see Uncle Isaiah, who was wearing his best suit. Ruth stared at him and said, 'How could Uncle Isaiah have crossed a river when he was sleeping?'

'Hush, child,' Grandma said, with tears streaming. 'Your Uncle Isaiah has gone home to Jesus.'

Uncle Isaiah was buried in the rain. People said his sins had been washed away. We children cried for days, but Grandma said it was a blessing, for Uncle Isaiah was in heaven now.

The following day, Grandma fed the pigs in the sty and I stood watching her. The ground shifted under our feet and I screamed: 'Grandma, Grandma, the earth is moving!'

She looked up at the sky, saying, 'It is an earth tremor. The heavens will open soon.'

I thought the sky would burst and the angels and God would come down from heaven. There was the sound of thunder, followed by lightning and I saw the limbs of a coconut tree crash to the ground with smoke rising.

'Lightning has struck the tree,' Grandma said, as the sky grew even darker and the rain fell even faster and steam rose from the ground.

We ran into the house where Grandpa and the others waited. He had earlier secured the other animals in their dwellings and locked Toby in his kennel. We children cowered as the thunder rolled, while Grandma told us the story of Noah and the Ark.

That night, we huddled in our grandparents' huge bed, with its mahogany headboard. Thunder clapped on the roof outside as we all sang: 'The Lord's my Shepherd, I'll not want . . .'

'Grandpa Noah,' Ruth said, 'with a name like yours, you must be blessed, so I know God will save us.'

Grandpa did not reply, but Grandma said, 'If Christ is in the vessel, He'll smile at the storm.'

'Toby, Toby,' Joshua said. 'I can hear him, barking.'

Grandpa rose, looking worried. He reached under the bed and took out his lasso. Then he peeped through the jalousie window. The storm was raging: trees bent and swayed as the wind howled and debris rushed along.

'I've got to get him out of the kennel!' Grandpa's voice sounded in the room. 'Before that cedar tree falls on top of it.' He struggled into his boots.

'You can't go out there, Noah,' Grandma said sternly. 'You'll surely die this night.'

'Grandpa, Grandpa,' we cried, 'please don't go out there!'

'Give me a hand, Rhoda,' Grandpa said. 'I'm going to tie this rope round my waist and attach it to something steady.'

Grandpa was in the sitting-room in a flash.

Then he secured the rope to one of the legs of the dining-table. He opened the door and the wind came in, blowing pictures down and curtains upwards. All the small ornaments crashed to the floor.

'Go back to bed, children,' Grandma said.

The table slowly slid across the room. It stopped at the narrow door and we gasped with relief. We were too afraid and excited to obey Grandma. We peered through the window, into the darkness, watching Grandpa tossing about like a rag doll.

'I don't want Grandpa to die,' Joshua said.

'Don't you know he's blessed?' Ruth said. 'God will save him. Wait and see.'

Grandma closed the window. Then she prayed openly, asking God to protect us. There was nothing she could do indoors, because as fast as she picked up ornaments the wind blew them down, hurling them against the wall.

'I've got him!' Grandpa shouted. 'Let me in.'

We helped to move the table. Then Grandpa came in, soaked to the skin and covered in mud. He had fallen several times. Poor Toby was also covered in mud. The zinc had blown off the roof of his kennel and he had sat in a corner, barking. He was whimpering and trembling as Grandpa cradled him, saying, 'All is well now, my pet.'

'Thank God you're all right,' Grandma said. 'Now let's wrap Toby in a sheet and put the children to bed.'

Thunderbolts sounded outside and we ran into the bedroom, screaming. Our grandparents knelt down at the bedside. They prayed like we had never heard them pray before and finally we fell asleep, confident that God was watching over us.

Next morning, the storm had passed. It had caused a lot of damage. Several banana trees had been uprooted. Breadfruit had fallen from trees, so had avocado pears and apples. Many coconut trees had lost their branches. The roof had blown off the chicken coop. Coffee trees were flattened and, as Grandpa had predicted, the cedar tree had crashed into Toby's kennel, which was beyond repair. The gutters that carried the rain-water had blown down and the red dirt in the yard had turned to mud. There were many insects lying still or squirming in the mud, along with leaves and paper. The scene brought tears to our eyes, even Grandma cried.

'Dry your eyes,' Grandpa ordered, holding Toby to his chest. 'At least we're all alive. We can repair the damage.'

'God be praised,' Grandma said.

I looked at Grandpa. He was stroking Toby and smiling as if the storm was but a dream. He was the bravest man I had ever known and his smile reminded me of someone. I suddenly wondered whether my father was as brave as Grandpa? I hoped that one day I would find that he was.

13

Treasures under the Tomb

Cousin Archie was a big man. He and Grandpa were first cousins. He had drooping eyelids and was toothless, since he rarely wore his false teeth. He had been to Panama and it was also whispered in the village that he had been to El Dorado. He was wise and mean, or so people said. His wife was called Aunt Jemima. For some reason, they had no children and rarely went out. They liked my company, so I visited them often.

Aunt Jemima was much fairer than Cousin Archie. She had thin lips and dark circles under her eyes. She wore her grey hair in a hairnet and her cheeks were lined with age. They were kind to me. One day, I sat on the verandah talking to Aunt Jemima, while Cousin Archie disappeared for some time.

'Hope,' Aunt Jemima said, when Cousin Archie returned, 'we want you to have this.'

My eyes widened when I saw gold flashing in the sun. Cousin Archie held out his hand and I took the thing: it was a gold pen and it was very cold, which seemed strange because we were perspiring in the heat as we drank homemade ginger ale.

'Thank you,' I said gratefully. 'I'm going to use this pen to write stories about my people and the land one day.'

'That's what we like to hear,' Cousin Archie and Aunt Jemima said at once. 'Nothing beats an ambitious child.'

When I arrived home, Grandma and Grandpa said: 'Hope, Archie and Jemima are very mean. They never give anything away. This is an honour. You must treasure it.'

I was proud of the pen and took it to Sunday school. The children passed it around, then gave it back to me. It fell from my hand and rolled into a hole between the floorboards.

'My gold pen!' I clawed at the boards with my bare hands until my nails broke and my fingers bled.

The Sunday school teacher, Miss Violet, glared at me, saying: 'Hope, toys should be left at home. This is the Lord's day.'

I looked at the floor, saying, 'That was not a toy. That was a real gold pen.' Then I continued searching, thinking: she's got that wrong, every day belongs to the Lord.

The next time I visited Cousin Archie and Aunt Jemima, I had to tell them about the pen. I felt dreadful. But all they said was, 'Never mind. We have something else for you.'

Cousin Archie was gone a long time while I

talked to Aunt Jemima. She wore her hair in a bun, secured with a hairnet as usual. She was making coconut cakes in the kitchen. I stared at her twisted hands as she struggled with a wooden spoon.

'We'll be eating coconut cakes for weeks,' Aunt Jemima said crossly. 'The storm destroyed all our coconut trees, and now they are limbless, not a branch in sight!' She shook her head. 'Sometimes it makes you wonder if God is sleeping!'

'Aunt Jemima!' I said. 'You're blaspheming. God never sleeps. He's always watching over us.'

'I wish I had your faith, child,' Aunt Jemima said. 'God has failed me so many times.'

'He never fails you if you pray earnestly,' I said.

'Ah, child,' Aunt Jemima said. 'Don't take everything you read in the Bible for gospel. It is written by man.'

Just then, Cousin Archie returned and the conversation ended. He held out a silver spoon. 'Hope, Jemima and I want you to have this.'

My eyes widened as I took the cold spoon and asked, 'Is it real silver?'

'Yes,' Aunt Jemima said. 'Archie brought it back all the way from Panama. He bought it for our child.'

'Child?' I said. 'But you have no children.'

'We had a son,' Cousin Archie said. 'He died

when he was a baby. We wanted more children, and we prayed constantly, but it was not to be. You are like the daughter we never had.'

At home, Grandma and Grandpa said, 'Hope, this spoon shows how much Archie and Jemima care for you. You must always treasure it.'

Ruth and Joshua said noisily: 'Cousin Archie and Aunt Jemima never invite us up to the big house. They're like most old people! They only like quiet children.' But they were not jealous for long.

One day, I sat in the sitting-room with Cousin Archie and Aunt Jemima, whose house was a sight to behold. There was a patterned rug on the polished floor and mahogany furniture in the dark sitting-room. The house was built in colonial style: a verandah took up the entire front of the impressive white mansion, the only one of its kind in our village. There was a kitchen, bathroom and a sitting-room downstairs and a creaking staircase led up to the bedrooms, where the doors opened on to a narrow balcony, from where you looked down on a fragrant rose garden. There were shutters protecting the glass windows from the changing weather, and mosquito netting round the large mahogany bed in which Cousin Archie and Aunt Jemima slept.

I sat looking at the patterned rug, wondering how Cousin Archie and Aunt Jemima could afford to live in such splendour. I thought the house was far too big for two people. But I was ashamed of myself when I recalled Grandpa saying how Cousin Archie, who was in his eighties, had toiled in horrendous conditions, working on the building of the Panama Canal in 1914.

Aunt Jemima read my thoughts. She said, 'Hope, Archie worked long and hard in Panama. He saved every penny to build this house, because he wanted us to have a comfortable life and lots of children. He gets a pension now, thank God. That is why we can afford to live in the style of the old colonials.'

'The bad old days.' Cousin Archie shuddered. 'I'm off to prune the roses.'

'Be careful of the thorns,' Aunt Jemima said. She was sewing a doll's dress but her hands shook as she worked, for she was arthritic. When she had finished, she said, 'Hope, I want you to have this.'

It was a china doll which had big brown eyes. It was wearing the dress Aunt Jemima had made. We joined Cousin Archie in the garden where an abundance of pink, red, yellow and white roses scented the air as the rhinestones from the doll's dress glittered in the sunlight.

'You look after that doll,' he said. 'I brought it back from Panama and the dress is made from a piece of material that was in the trunk.' His large frame seemed shrunken. He snipped a red rose and there was a faraway look in his eyes as he gave the rose to Aunt Jemima.

'Do you mean the trunk with the treasures that you brought back from El Dorado?' I asked, holding the doll to my chest.

'Lord, child,' Aunt Jemima said, sniffing the rose. 'El Dorado is a mythical city and we have no treasures.'

'What about the treasures that are supposed to be hidden in the trunk?' I asked.

Cousin Archie placed an arm around Aunt Jemima's shoulders and said, 'I brought back a trunk from Panama. It contained my clothes and souvenirs.'

At home, Grandma and Grandpa said, 'Hope, you look after that doll. See how delicate and beautiful it is.'

On my birthday, Aunt Jemima spent the day baking. We all ate ginger cake and drank lemonade. Then we talked about my father. I was curious; I couldn't imagine him being a boy.

'Hope,' Cousin Archie said, 'you're quiet, just like your father was at your age. He would sit on the verandah, reading the newspaper and discussing current affairs with Jemima and me. He wanted to be a journalist. He should have gone to college when he left school. Instead he got a low-down job in a sweetie factory in Kingston.'

'Now, now, Archie,' Aunt Jemima said. 'Don't forget: the boy ended up being deputy manager of that same factory.'

'Aunt Jemima,' I said, 'I can't understand why it's taking Mother and Father so long to send for us children. They've been gone for almost four years. I thought they loved us?'

'They do,' she said in a calm voice. 'But nothing is ever done before it's time.'

'What does that mean?' I asked.

'You must learn to be patient,' Cousin Archie said.

'This is for you.' Aunt Jemima handed me a cameo brooch.

Cousin Archie put in his false teeth. 'I brought it back from Panama as a homecoming gift for Jemima.'

That evening, Grandma and Grandpa admired the brooch. 'Hope, Archie and Jemima are not as mean as people think,' they said. 'It is an honour to receive such a beautiful trinket. You must always treasure it.'

One day, Cousin Archie said it was time I shared their secret. I followed him and Aunt Jemima into the graveyard at the other end of their land; their only son and Cousin Archie's parents were buried there. (That was where Cousin Archie had disappeared to on the occasions when he'd returned with the gold pen and the silver spoon.) My knees knocked and my legs trembled as I stared at the lonely graves. I closed my eyes when Cousin Archie began to dig. There was the creaking of a lid and he said,

'Let's see what I've unearthed.'

'Open your eyes.' Aunt Jemima held a silver knife and fork, saying: 'Now you have the set. All that is left of the souvenirs that Archie brought back from Panama. They are treasured memories and special, just like you.'

'When I was a boy,' Cousin Archie said, 'I dreamed of finding buried treasures. I suppose I've fulfilled my dream.' Then he added: 'Hope, this is our secret. Let the people continue thinking that we've buried the treasures on the land.'

Aunt Jemima's face seemed to sag. She handed me the knife and fork, saying: 'Some day Archie and I will be gone, and you will be joining your parents in England, but we hope you will remember us by these tokens.'

'I'll never forget you,' I said very quietly because I was almost in tears. 'I don't want you to die.'

'Hope,' Cousin Archie seemed to drag out my name, and his voice deepened, 'death is a release for old people. We have lived our lives. Now it is your turn. When you leave this village, go forth confidently: no tears or tantrums when it's time to say goodbye to your grandparents.'

Aunt Jemima placed a thin arm around my shoulders. 'Archie and I expect you to do a lot better than your father, Hope.' She tucked the rose behind my ear and cuddled me.

'I'll try,' I said, looking up at Cousin Archie

and Aunt Jemima. They seemed to have aged drastically in seconds. When we said goodbye that afternoon I sensed that I would not see them again.

14

Dominic

I had just got over the death of Cousin Archie when Aunt Jemima followed. Grandpa said I needed cheering up, so did Ruth and Joshua, who were for ever asking about our parents now. Grandpa announced that we could go on a pet-buying spree with Grandma.

It was a bright Saturday morning when we boarded the bus at the crossroads. First of all, women squabbled about who should lead the singsong but naturally, they chose Grandma as they knew she had the best voice. They sang 'Onward, Christian soldiers', followed by a folk song and their voices filled the lonely country road as they rocked and swayed, singing:

'Carry me ackee go a Linstead Market,
Not a quatty wut sell.
Carry me ackee go a Linstead Market,
Not a quatty wut sell.
Lard, wat a night, not a bite,
Wat a satiday night . . .
Lard, wat a night, not a bite,
Wat a satiday night . . .

Everybody come feel up, feel up,
Not a quatty wut sell.
Everybody come feel up, feel up,
Not a quatty wut sell.
Lard, wat a night, not a bite,
Wat a satiday night . . .
Mek me call i' louder: ackee! ackee!
Red an' pretty dem tan!
Lady, buy yu Sunday marnin' brukfas',
Rice an' ackee nyam gran'.
Lard, wat a night, not a bite,
Wat a satiday night . . .
All de pickney dem a linga, linga,
Fe weh dem mumma no bring.
All de pickney dem a linga, linga,
Fe weh dem mumma no bring.
Lard, wat a night, not a bite,
Wat a satiday night . . .'

At the market, we saw women sitting on benches. They had baskets on the ground, selling fruit and vegetables of different colours while trying to out-shout each other.

The men pushed barrels and rounded up the animals, shouting, 'Hey, man. Come spen' some money wid me nuh. Buy me goats, sah!' Others shouted, 'Hey, sah. Buy me pigs nuh!

'Lady, don't be like dat,' one of the women shouted. 'Come an' buy me chickens nuh! Yuh cayn hide-up all de money in de thread-bag like dat, mam!'

'Peanuts! Peanuts . . .' some of the children shouted, while others pushed barrels, selling ice-shavings – crushed ice with strawberry syrup on top.

After Grandma had sold the eggs and vegetables, she said, 'Children, it's time to choose your pets.'

'Hi, lady. Come an' buy me hens nuh, mam!' shouted a thin bird-like woman. She clucked and flapped her arms like wings.

There was a coop of clucking hens. I saw a black, speckled hen fighting with the brown, white and black hens in the tiny coop. 'That's the one, Grandma,' I said, pointing.

'We have enough hens on the farm,' Grandma said. 'Choose another pet. How about a kitten?'

'Can I have a kitten, please?' Joshua asked.

'May I have a tortoise?' Ruth said.

Grandma was impatient today. She wanted us to buy the pets quickly, have lunch, then make our way back to the bus to get seats. It was uncomfortable standing in the aisle. People pushed and cursed when it was their turn to get off the bus.

'Please, Grandma,' I said. 'I don't want any other pet.'

'Very well,' Grandma said. 'But I still think you should have chosen a kitten. They are so round and cuddly.' Her face took on a big smile as she stared at several kittens miaowing. But she bought me the black speckled hen. By then

Joshua had chosen a kitten, a white, fluffy bundle. Ruth chose a tortoise. Then we had lunch and headed for the bus station.

Next day, Grandpa said, 'The hen needs a name.'

'Dominic,' I said. 'I'm going to call her Dominic.' This was because Grandma had said the breed came from Dominica.

Ruth named her tortoise Archie. Joshua named his kitten Jemima. But they did not get on with Dominic; she pecked Archie's back constantly. The poor tortoise rarely peeped out from under his shell. Jemima was not afraid of Dominic. She scratched at her eyes, so Dominic kept away from the kitten.

Grandma had a white hen, called Nesta, who was the leader of the other hens and also the successor to Frizzle. She patrolled the farm, squawking whenever hawks or mongeese appeared. Unfortunately, Dominic fought with Nesta and the other hens daily. There were always feathers flying; Dominic lost the most.

'Dominic is the first bald-headed hen on this farm,' Grandpa said, one morning. 'We'll have to make her a coop.'

With each passing week, Dominic lost more and more feathers, fighting with the hens and roosters. She also tried to crow like the roosters, climbing on top of their coop.

'Hope, you should have got a kitten, like Joshua,' Grandma said. 'It would have been well trained by now.'

One day, the roosters were fighting in the yard. Dominic joined in. All four turned on her. When they had finished, Dominic had lost so many feathers that Grandpa said she looked as though she had been plucked for roasting.

'Dominic thinks she's a rooster,' Grandma said. 'It's time we mated her.'

At first I thought Grandma meant it was time Dominic had a friend. I said, 'Dominic doesn't need a mate. She has me.'

Grandpa laughed and said, 'When you are older, you will understand.' Grandpa had a new pet, too. Aunt Enid could not look after Cheyenne any more so she gave him to Grandpa. Cheyenne had taken to Grandpa the day Grandpa found him guarding Uncle Isaiah in the field. And he kept on straying to our farm. Toby followed Grandpa as he rode off on Cheyenne, saying, 'I'm going to get some timber and mesh wire to make a coop for Dominic.'

The coop was built, but Dominic refused to go inside. Instead she sat on top, preening her feathers. Then she began to disappear for long spells. One day, she simply vanished and I assumed that hawks or mongeese had taken her, because she was a loner. Nesta and the other hens stuck together, and could be seen cackling and running towards their coop whenever they sensed danger.

Dominic had been gone for over a month. We

children walked the length of the farm, calling out her name, but she could not be found. I was very upset and I cried for days. It seemed my pet had been stolen by a hawk or a mongoose, just like Grandma's favourite hen, Frizzle.

'Hope,' Grandma said, 'you are a big girl now. It's time you stopped acting like a cry baby.'

We were sitting on the verandah and Ruth said, 'Grandma, can I take Archie to school? The headmaster has a tortoise called Shelley. They can keep each other company.'

In truth, Grandma did not mind, for Ruth was neglecting Archie. She preferred braiding her hair with the red, white and blue ribbons which Mother had sent in the latest parcel. So Archie went to live with Mr Trelawny and Shelley.

A few weeks later, Dominic came into the yard, clucking, with several chicks in tow.

'Dominic is a mother now,' Grandma said. 'She's been mating secretly with one of the roosters.' She looked at me and added, 'Hope, a hen with a brood is no longer a pet.'

'It's just as well the coop is finished,' Grandpa said. 'Let's put the chicks in the coop now.'

At first Dominic would not go into the coop and pecked anyone that went near her chicks. But eventually Grandpa chased her off and placed the chicks in the coop. Then Dominic quietly followed and they all settled down. I was sad because I had lost my pet.

Dominic had had ten chicks, yet I had never seen her mate. A few days later, I said: 'Grandma, where do babies come from and are all mothers protective of their children?'

Grandma did not reply for just then Grandpa rode into the yard at full speed. Cheyenne's breathing was audible and I swallowed saliva; I was still afraid of the horse. But Ruth and Joshua fed Cheyenne with wet sugar and led him round and round until Grandpa said we should go and sit on the verandah. His face looked drawn, so I knew something bad had happened.

'What is the problem?' Grandma asked, staring at Dominic and her chicks in the coop.

'Not in front of the children,' Grandpa said. He and Grandma walked around the yard, with their hands behind their backs, looking gravely at each other as they spoke.

Finally, our grandparents joined us on the verandah. Ruth sat fiddling with her ribbons. Joshua played with his kitten. Grandma adjusted her glasses. Grandpa stood holding a letter bearing a stamp with the face of the Queen. Then Joshua said, 'Grandpa, Grandpa, will you do a jig for me? You haven't danced for ages.'

'This is the last time,' Grandpa said, but his legs failed him. It was as if the strength had left his body. He sat down and said, 'Children, there's news from England.'

I noticed that Grandpa's voice was different, almost tearful. Grandma cleared her throat and sucked in her bottom lip as she rocked in her chair. I studied Grandma's pained expression. I realized that the happiness we all shared would soon end.

15

Hope Leaves Jamaica

'Children, your days in the country are numbered,' Grandpa said. He had stopped at the post office. There was a letter from our parents. They had finally booked our air tickets. We were to fly to England in three months' time.

Grandma disappeared into the sitting-room. She returned and handed Grandpa a glass of rum punch. The kitten miaowed and purred as Grandma said slowly, 'Children, you have a baby sister in England.'

'That's impossible,' I said. 'Where did she come from?'

'Just think, you'll be with your parents at last,' Grandma said, hoarsely, ignoring my question. 'Isn't that good news?'

'How can it be good news?' Ruth asked. 'We are leaving you and Grandpa.'

'I asked my teacher to show me England on the map months ago,' Joshua said. 'I wanted to see where Mother and Father lived. Grandpa, you should have told me the truth. I would have understood.' Then he said, 'I don't want to go, Grandpa. I want to stay here with you and

Grandma for ever!'

'We'll always be here for you, Joshua,' Grandpa said. 'We never told you that your parents were abroad, because we didn't want you to fret too much.'

'I see,' Joshua said, stroking Jemima without enthusiasm.

I remembered my promise to Cousin Archie: no tears or tantrums when it was time to leave my grandparents. Of course, there would be no tantrums, but I couldn't stop the tears from flowing. I was devastated!

The weeks ahead passed in confusion. We were escorted to Kingston several times. We had to have passports as well as a thorough medical check-up. Meantime, the news spread throughout the village, for Grandpa had read the letter while standing outside the post office. But the villagers were tactful. They never mentioned our impending departure, because they knew that we would break down and weep in public. However, the Sunday school teacher, Miss Violet, presented us with a book of sacred songs, signed by all the children.

The time of our departure drew near and the pastor visited us at home. He said he would miss our obedient faces in church. He blessed us, saying: 'Children, take the name of Jesus with you; He will comfort you always.'

Grandpa said the pastor was not so bad after all. He had prayed with us at home to spare

Grandma the anguish of singing at another farewell service.

Uncle Ely and Aunt Esmé also came to see us. They said, sadly, 'Give Robin our love and God go with you.'

Aunt Enid arrived crying. She said, 'Children, Jehovah will guide you over the ocean.' She had received a letter from her son Samuel. He was coming home on vacation.

On our last day at school, the headmaster organised a special assembly. The children crowded round Ruth and Joshua, trying to touch their hands and faces, saying: 'Give Robin Redbreast our love and don't forget your old friends!'

In the assembly hall, the older children sang: 'The day thou gavest, Lord, is ended . . .', 'Land of our birth we pledge to Thee, our love and toil in the years to be . . .', followed by 'Now the day is over, Night is drawing nigh . . .'

When the singing ended, Mr Trelawny said: 'Children, you are marching on from childhood towards the blessed sunny slopes of life; seize opportunity by the hand, so that one day you can return to Jamaica as successful adults.'

I could not imagine leaving Jamaica, let alone returning as an adult. I wanted to be a child for ever. Just then the younger children began to sing 'My Bonny lies over the ocean'.

Parents who lived near the school, had come to the assembly – many were in tears. We brought tears to a lot of eyes for we were well known in the surrounding villages, because Grandma and Grandpa had lots of distant relatives.

The farewell ended. A horn sounded at the school gate. We walked down the steps, which no longer seemed scary. I was sad and Miss Clover walked me to the gate, saying: 'Hope, may your life be happy and all your days be bright . . .'

My eyes filled up with tears and when I opened my mouth to speak, the words just stuck in my throat.

'Grandpa, Grandpa.' Joshua went running. Ruth followed him and they shouted, 'Grandpa has come to collect us!'

In the past, we had begged Grandpa to collect us from school, but he was too busy on the farm. Today was exceptional. He stood by the bakery van with the words United Bakeries written on the side. He opened his arms and Ruth and Joshua flung themselves on to him.

The driver, Mr Brown, opened the sliding door, smiling. He had lost all his hair now. His gold tooth glistened in the sun as he handed us each a small paper bag. The children banged on the side of the van as we slowly moved off, eating freshly baked Jamaican buns.

Next day, we walked around the farm, saying goodbye to the animals. It was as if we had always lived there, because now we could not remember the day we had first arrived when Father had left us. Toby whimpered and we clung to him. Cheyenne neighed and Ruth and Joshua patted him, but I would still not go near him. Dominic and her brood were scratching near the coop. She sensed that something was wrong, for she flew on top of the coop and there she stood clucking, with her small eyes opening and closing. Then Joshua refused to part with Jemima, so Grandpa had to prize her away and she was given to Aunt Esmé.

Uncle Ely was the only man in the village with a car. We squeezed into the Austin Cambridge, stopping in the village square where we got out, trembling with excitement and fear.

A group of farmers rode past, saying: 'Children, we don't envy you, for this time tomorrow you'll be shivering!'

Man-Man and Big-Man appeared with Jubal. But our grandparents remained in the car. The villagers said goodbye to us while Grandpa stared ahead, ignoring Jubal, so he was led back to the corral by Man-Man and Big-Man.

We left the village behind, travelling up the winding mountain road, which no longer terrified us. We stared down at huge boulders of rocks, trembling ferns, burnt-out vehicles in the ravines and the ancient trees that spread their branches like canopies. We silently took it all in and a new dread took hold of us: England!

The road led downward and the countryside

was behind us. Finally, we crossed the famous Flat Bridge, in the parish of St Catherine, and Grandpa stared at the Rio Cobre river, saying, 'Rhoda, we're crossing that bridge at last.'

Grandma sniffed while Joshua said: 'Don't worry, Grandpa. When I'm a big man, I'm coming back to help you on the farm.'

'When I grow up,' Ruth said, 'I'm going to be the headmistress of my old school.'

'Anything is possible.' Grandma blew her nose. 'You are going to the land of opportunity.'

Uncle Ely was silent throughout. He was probably thinking about the same journey that he'd made with Robin. When we reached the airport, Grandma produced three handkerchiefs.

'Those are Father's handkerchiefs.' Ruth narrowed her eyes in confusion. 'I thought I had lost them.'

'I put them away for safe keeping,' Grandma said, handing us each a handkerchief. 'I want you children to wave them when you reach the top step of the aeroplane.'

'Children,' Grandpa said, 'this is the last time I'm going to advise you: "labour for learning before you grow old, for learning is better than silver and gold".'

'Your grandpa is right,' Grandma said, smiling. Then she added, 'Children, never forget: "silver and gold will vanish away, but a good education will never decay".'

All the children who left our village received the same advice from teachers or elders. Nevertheless, the words terrified us, for we knew deep down that our promise had to be fulfilled, otherwise we would be letting down our grandparents. Also, we had said too many goodbyes and now words failed us.

Grandpa spoke again: 'Children, there is nothing more for us to give you, except our love. That you know you will have for ever.' Then he and Grandma hugged us really hard.

I felt like a miniature adult when Uncle Ely shook my hand and said: 'Hope, be good and look after the children.'

When we reached the top step of the aeroplane, we stood waving along with many others, though we couldn't see our grandparents. We boarded the aeroplane with tears streaming. Poor Joshua could hardly walk; his legs were trembling so badly. Ruth sobbed into her handkerchief while a yellow-haired stewardess fastened our seat belts and moved off.

The aeroplane sped down the runway. It zoomed upwards and I braced myself, staring down at the blue Caribbean Sea. Meantime, Ruth and Joshua shook with fear. I pleated the handkerchief, thinking, Hope, stop acting like a cry baby. So I dried my eyes and thought about my parents and our life ahead. Then I said to myself, 'We're going to be together at last, but what will the future hold?'

Glossary

Ackee	A yellow fruit, though eaten as a vegetable
Anancy	Brer Anancy inspires many stories about how he triumphs over bigger and stronger animals by using his wits
Annatto	A spice, brick-red in colour, rather like paprika
Blue Mahoe	National tree – has blue-green colour with variegated yellow intrusion – valuable source of cabinet timber
Breadfruit	A large fruit with green outer skin and yellow interior, eaten as a vegetable – can be boiled or roasted
Bulla cake	Small cake made with flour, molasses and soya
Calaban	A manmade trap with a noose – used to catch animals
Cho-cho	A vegetable, lightish green in colour
Corn-pone	Similar to bread pudding
Duppy-story	Ghost-story
Grip	An old-fashioned suitcase
Guinep	A fruit – green skin, rather like a shell – has a fleshy, peach-coloured interior – it grows in bunches
Higgler	Market trader

Johnchewit	A smallish, white-bellied bird – sings the word "johnchewit" as it searches for food, hence it is called Johnchewit
Johnny cake	Dumpling
Jonkonnu	Procession masquerading in streets, during the Christmas and New Year celebrations, wearing flamboyant costumes
Kingstonian	A person who was born in Kingston
Mulatto	A person who has one black and one white parent
Naseberry	A fleshy fruit with lots of brown seeds – very sweet and has a soft brown skin
Okra	A vegetable – listed in the dictionary
Poinciana tree	Tree with spreading branches, bearing an abundance of red flowers
Polly lizard	A small dark lizard, generally found in houses
Quadroon	A person who is one quarter black
Quatty	Jamaican word for penny-half-penny
Red ants	Ants that are red in colour, marching round and round like soldiers
Ska	A popular dance during the Sixties
Sweetsop	A sweet, pulpy fruit – listed in the dictionary
Tank	A large, concrete, man-made water container

Creole	Standard English
Bwoy	Boy
Breddas/Broddas	Brothers
Brukfus'	Breakfast
Busha	An overseer
Chile	Child
Cho!	Interjection – Pshaaw!
Cyan/cahn	Can't
Das/Dat's	That is
Dat	That
De	The
Dem	Them
Dese	These
Dis	This
Dung	Down
Eberyting	Everything
Fe	For
Finga/s	Finger/s
Gal	Girl
Gwine	Going

Creole	Standard English
Howdy-do	Howdy/Hello
Lard	Lord
Maddah	Mother
Mas	Mr
Me	I/My
Mek/Meck	Make
Mek-Mekin'	Fussing
'Merica	America
Nuh	No/Now
Nyam	Eat
Pickney/s	Child/Children
Sah	Sir
Sinting	Something
Tief	Thief
Thread-bag	Draw-string purse
Wat	What
Wata	Water
Wid	With
Wo't'/Wut	Worth
Yu/Yuh	You